MARRIED TO THE PLAYBOY

TONI DENISE

1

"You have got to be joking." Kristen only barely stopped herself from stomping her foot.

"It is what it is," Principal Jenkins told her. "The play isn't going to happen unless we get some people in the community to help and a teacher to coordinate it."

"I already do a lot. There are other teachers you could ask to help." She knew she was whining but it seemed every time something needed doing, she was the only one that anyone asked. She also had a hard time saying no and everyone knew it.

"The fifth-grade teachers are busy preparing their graduation, so if we want the annual play to happen, we need someone who knows what needs to be done. You helped Mrs. Kline for two years before she retired, so you know what to do," he explained.

It was true she knew what needed to happen, but that didn't change the fact that she had other things to do already and that she wasn't even the one who volunteered for this in the first place.

"Why can't Beth do it?" Beth, a third-grade teacher, had volunteered to at the beginning of the school year.

Kristen had ended up with the majority of Beth's duties since she started there as a teacher last year. Somehow, she had everyone convinced she was too nice and also too weak to do her own work. Beth hated Kristen though and had ever since they'd met. She had no idea why.

Kristen had asked her once, only for Beth to laugh right in her face, instead of giving her an answer. It was one of very few times that, outside of her brother, Kristen had truly wanted to punch someone, preferably in the face, breaking her perfect little nose.

"Well, she's just really overwhelmed."

Kristen felt her jaw drop. "She quit on it?"

"I didn't say that." He did though, it was written all over his face, if not in his words. "Look, I'm just asking for your help," He took a deep breath and went in for the kill, sealing Kristen's fate, "The kids need your help."

"It's a month away!" She crossed her arms and huffed. "It's not going to be the same as when Mrs. Kline did it; it takes a whole year to plan." A thought crossed her mind, "Beth hasn't done anything, has she?" She pointed her finger at the principal.

"I'm afraid not." Principal Jenkins shook his head. To his credit he did at least look disappointed.

"It'll be different and I don't know what I can pull off."

"I'm just asking that you do your best." He smiled at her before adding, "That's all the kids ask for."

"You've already got me, so you can stop laying it on so thick." Not even trying to stop herself, she rolled her eyes. "She's doing my bus duties for the rest of the year." It was a statement, not a question.

"Now, I don't know if I can have her do it for that—"

Kristen cut him off with a look. "I need time to coordinate all of this." She threw her arms wide.

Nodding, he relented. "Consider it covered."

She put her hand on the doorknob to leave, but had a thought. "This is the only time. I'm going to stop being the teacher here all day every day after this. You better ask the rest of your staff to step up."

She didn't turn around to see his reaction, instead leaving the door open as she walked away. Trying to show power in the conversation that she definitely did not have control over, and also scared that if she turned around he would call her bluff.

It was the end of the school day, so the halls were empty except for a few lingering teachers and staff. Almost always, Kristen was one of the first ones in and definitely one of the last ones out of Springfield Elementary School. Most days she enjoyed the extra things she did, but recently she was growing restless.

It probably had something to do with her brother getting married and having a stepson, with a baby on the way. When she gave herself time to think about it, she realized she was jealous, but she didn't like that, so she didn't give herself much time to think about it.

When she got back to her classroom, she pulled out her phone and called Macy, her sister-in-law.

"Hey girl, I'm not going to make it tonight."

"No, you are not backing out; you need to leave work."

Kristen smiled, thinking of the quiet girl that she'd originally met. Macy had really found herself since getting with Daniel, Kristen's brother. Turned out Macy liked to be in charge and was really good at it.

"I have a new project, doing the entire end-of-year show."

"It can wait until tomorrow. You are coming tonight for dinner."

"Macy, I appreciate it, but I can't."

"Bull. You can and you will; you cancel every time these days."

"Macy—"

"Please, Kristen? We haven't seen you in forever. And I want to talk to you too." She could almost hear Macy's wheels turning, before she continued, "I'll come over and help you with whatever it is tomorrow?"

"I appreciate the offer, but I need to figure out what I am doing first."

"Come on, please?"

"Okay, I will come tonight."

"Yay! You'll feel good to step away from work for a bit."

"I'm not staying long."

"Sure." They both knew she wasn't agreeing to anything though.

Kristen was going to do her best to leave at a decent time to get home and start planning. Sighing as she packed up her work, she knew Macy would convince her to stay, and it wouldn't take much effort even; she needed to work on saying no and holding her ground.

Glancing down at her outfit, she considered going home to change but then dismissed that idea. That would definitely say she planned on being there for a while. Her black pants and paint-stained blouse would have to do.

Despite Beth and all the other stressful things that went along with being a teacher, she loved her kids. It was great seeing the kids grow for the year, and being a second-grade teacher, she got to see the kids grow until the end of fifth grade.

Her class was lively. It annoyed some parents when they found out she didn't have strict desk rules or loads of homework, but that was fine. The kids could sit at a desk, or in a bean bag, or lay on the rug, whatever they needed to do to get the work done. She'd made it through college often laid across her bed, and it had worked well for her.

"Kristen?"

She froze at the voice before turning towards her door. Beth was standing there looking as freshly put together as she had at the beginning of the day. Clearly not a stressful Friday for her. Not a platinum-blonde hair out of place, high heels clicking across the hard floor as she walked in, her black pencil skirt and nearly see-through blouse were just this side of respectable.

"Can I help you?" Kristen asked and then mentally kicked herself. She didn't want to help Beth with anything, definitely the wrong question to ask.

"I'm glad you asked." The smile was sweet but Beth's blue eyes held contempt. "I heard you wanted me to take your bus duties, and I just can't."

"Excuse me?" That was it? Just can't? We aren't even going to make up an excuse anymore?

"Yeah, you'll need to keep doing them." She started walking away.

"Why not?" Kristen asked.

"I have personal reasons." Beth gave a little smile, but it wasn't friendly.

"You expect me to do all of your work?"

Beth laughed her sweet, fake, feminine laugh and didn't answer as she walked away. Kristen wanted to yell out in frustration but didn't. She opened her top desk drawer and pulled out a self-help book about learning to say no and added it to her bag.

"This weekend I will read you," she thought out loud as she picked her bag up and left the school.

She was all the way to her car before she wondered why dinner was so important tonight. The car was in gear and she was on her way there before she allowed herself to admit there was only one reason why Macy would push so hard.

"Mike," she said before groaning. Not one to curse normally, there was only one word to sum up the situation: "Shit."

It was definitely going to be a long night and Macy better have thought to grab some wine, because that was the only way Kristen was going to get through it.

2

———

The drive to Daniel and Macy's was nearly an hour from his own house, and Mike was exhausted. He had considered bailing but was looking forward to a home-cooked dinner and some friendly faces. So instead, after a long day of construction on the home he was building for a client and he went home, took a long shower to clean himself up, and headed out.

The saddest part was that the job site was closer to Daniel's, but there was no way he could have shown up like that. As hot as it was today, he had been gross. Before Daniel and Macy had gotten together, he wouldn't have cared—well he might have if Kristen was coming—but generally it was just them and Daniel certainly didn't care.

But now he was trekking out of his way to get cleaned up. He had packed a bag and considered showering at Daniel's but that didn't seem right with Macy living there now.

Macy had told him that Kristen was definitely coming tonight, and that had motivated him to stop at the store now. If he knew Kristen, which he liked to think he did, she was going to want a glass of wine on a Friday night, having likely been guilted into coming if he knew anything.

Kristen had avoided him for nearly a year now. It had taken him months to get her to admit why and he couldn't believe it. Apparently, he'd had a one-night stand with her friend Rebecca and she was upset with him.

He'd figured she would get over it eventually, unsure if she was mad on her friend's behalf or jealous too. He'd hoped she had a little jealousy but the longer she stayed mad at him the more that hope faded. She wouldn't even talk to him to let him explain.

Not that he had much to explain. They were adults, and the friend, he hadn't even slept with her. He'd taken the chick home and decided she was too drunk and that he wasn't in the mood. She'd gotten mad at him and started spreading that rumor.

Truth was, while he knew he had charm, he did flirt with women, lots of them, but any he slept with he stayed with. one-night stands were something he never did as a personal rule. If Kristen would just let him talk to her, he might be able to get her to believe the truth. Or she'd accuse him of lying.

He'd even looked up the friend, Laurel, and called her out on the lie. She'd went off on him instead, saying it was his fault that he didn't follow through and that she'd not lied, only implied and let people take it from there. He'd threatened to spread his own rumors about her, but she knew he wasn't going to do it, so they were at an impasse.

There didn't seem to be any real way out of the mess, outside of convincing Kristen that he was telling the truth. Something that for the last year had been impossible, aside from just screaming it at her, but more recently he hadn't even seen her enough to do that.

Tonight, he was going to try again to talk to her. He was going to get her favorite wine to get things started, and with that and Macy's help, he had a small chance at getting her attention for a few minutes. Macy had listened and believed him, but he'd wanted to talk to Kristen before he got anyone else involved.

He wasn't quite sure why Macy had taken an interest in helping him. She was definitely more Kristen's friend than his, but he appreciated it. She was definitely meddling, but right now he needed the help.

He smiled and picked up a bouquet of flowers. Flowers usually helped smooth things over. He grabbed a second bouquet for Macy too: he didn't want to scare Kristen by singling her out.

He hadn't been interested in her at first. He'd met her while on leave with Daniel, but she wasn't his type. A little nerdy and a lot too nice for him. At the time, Mike met his women at bars, and he preferred them just as outgoing as himself, and into casual relationships.

Kristen was a commitment, and Mike had decided in the time since he'd left the army that he wanted to settle down eventually. Daniel's injury had scared him into thinking about his own future, and the more he got to know her, the more Mike wanted Kristen in that future.

Deciding at the last minute that maybe two bottles of wine would be better, he ran and grabbed a second bottle of her favorite moscato and a twelve-pack of beer for him and Daniel to drink as well. Macy wouldn't be drinking as she had found out she was pregnant not that long ago.

"Hey, darlin'" the cashier greeted as he put his wine and flowers on the belt.

Mike flashed a grin. "How are you?"

"I'm good." She smiled back and toyed with her necklace, not scanning his items. "You got a hot date?" She gestured to his items.

"Something like that." He grabbed a pack of sour gummy candy from the shelf for Chris, Macy's brother and one of Kristen's students, and added a chocolate bar for Macy, just so everyone got something.

"Seems like a lucky woman. If it doesn't work out, I get off at ten." She winked at him and scanned his stuff.

He paid and left, not giving her a second thought. His mind was focused on getting Kristen to listen to him. Tonight was the night, God willing. If he could get her to listen to him just once, then he'd at least be able to say he'd tried.

He wasn't totally stuck on the idea of Kristen at first. He'd tried, hard, to start other relationships, but they hadn't gone anywhere. Everything came back to her, and he wanted to at least explore that possibility. He'd also decided that if he couldn't break the ice with her tonight, at least a little, that he needed to move on and that might mean staying away from Daniel's for a bit until he could get Kristen off his mind.

Pulling up at Daniel's, he noticed that Kristen's car wasn't here yet. He hoped she didn't back out again tonight. The last few times they'd all tried to get together, Kristen had been too busy. Unfortunately, part of that busy was definitely her avoiding him.

After a moment's debate about leaving everything in the truck, he grabbed it all and went inside.

"Honey, I'm home," he yelled, after letting himself in.

"Shut up," Daniel called from the kitchen.

"I come bearing gifts though." He set the bags and the beer on the table.

"Guess you can stay then," Daniel said immediately, opening the box and grabbing a bottle. "Macy didn't get any beer for tonight, glad you remembered."

He didn't say it out loud, but Mike was certain she hadn't forgotten.

"Those for me?" Daniel asked pointing at the flowers.

"Had I known you wanted some, I would have grabbed you one too." Mike opened his own beer and took a long pull.

"They must be for me. Two single men gotta look out for each other, you know?" David said as he walked in.

David was the third man in their friend group who also served with them. He was the joking one where Daniel was silent and Mike charmed everyone. His dark brown hair was always shaved and he had a constant 5 o'clock shadow. He was more muscular than Mike, but had a way of making himself seem small in certain situations despite the fact that he was larger than almost anyone in the room, always.

"I do like to be charmed every now and then," Daniel joked.

"Who all is coming tonight?" Mike asked, trying to sound casual.

"Just you, him, and Kristen."

Mike nodded, trying not to be too happy about the confirmation that she was coming. He took in Daniel, who looked so much better than he had in years since getting together with Macy. "Where's Macy?"

"Helping Chris do his homework."

"Kristen is a hard teacher, homework on a Friday?"

They laughed, knowing that she wasn't. "Some project she assigned them, and Macy won't let it wait until Sunday. Plus, since the teacher will be here shortly, he can ask any questions."

"Sure, he will, definitely not Macy," Mike said with sarcasm.

"I'll leave these here then until Macy comes to join us." He put the flowers on the counter and the wine in the fridge. "You remembered all the alcohol tonight, huh? Trying to get my sister drunk with two bottles just for her."

Mike shrugged one shoulder. "They were on sale." They weren't, but Daniel didn't know that.

"Clearly, Mike has completely forgotten that your wife is pregnant." David made a show of winking and elbowing Mike.

"Shut up," Mike said, and stepped on his foot as he walked away, trying to inflict a little pain.

"Nope, steel toe, didn't feel a thing." David laughed.

"What's the deal between you two anyway? What's she so mad about?" Daniel questioned, as he had time and again.

"You keep asking and I keep telling you it's between us."

"And since you haven't answered, I have to keep asking." Daniel set his beer on the table and got serious for a moment. "You better not have messed around with her. I swear if I find out—"

"Whoa!" Mike held up his hands in surrender. "It's nothing like that; it's just between us. I'm trying to talk to her and clear some stuff up, but she hasn't exactly been cooperative."

"If you told me what it was, I could talk to her."

"Look, I just want to speak for myself, I need her to hear it from me." He still didn't really know why he was happy to accept help from Macy to get them in the same room again, but not help with the situation itself, other than he needed to explain himself and wanted to be the one to do it.

"Fine, you two keep your secrets." Daniel downed the rest of his beer and stood.

"When are we expecting her anyway?" Mike asked.

"Anytime now. She tried to back out, but Macy laid it on thick with her." Daniel laughed. "It's usually pretty easy to get Kristen to say yes."

Mike had noticed that about her in the time he'd known her. Kristen was always quick to help anyone even when you could see she didn't really want to. A lot of people took advantage of that.

"Macy said she got assigned the end-of-year play for the kids today," Daniel told him.

"I don't know much about those things, but it seems a little late in the year to do that, doesn't it?"

Daniel just shrugged as Macy joined them. "You guys can get the grill going. Kristen should be here any time now, and I'll get the salad made when the macaroni comes out of the oven."

"Hi, Macy." Mike handed her the flower and gave her a kiss on the cheek. "I missed you."

"You snake charmer. Go start the grill." Macy swatted him but started unwrapping the flowers.

"You heard her, let's go." Mike opened the door and held it for Daniel who was recovering from another surgery on his leg and was still using a cane for support, letting go as David started to walk out the door.

"Knew it was coming," David taunted.

David was always happy. Mike didn't think he'd once seen him sour, and even when Daniel was wounded, it was David trying to lighten the mood and take everyone's mind off the subject. He had gotten out when Mike did and stuck around mostly near town.

More often than not though, he was out of town. Traveling for work as a security consultant, where, apparently, he was very serious and highly respected. Which didn't fit with the friend he knew most of the time. He could be serious, sure, he'd been in enough tough situations with him to know he wasn't a total goof, but those moments were rare.

Mike was comfortable around the grill and moving in and out of their kitchen with ease. He'd been here so many times he didn't have to ask where anything was. Macy had moved a few things around when she moved in, but in a way that made more sense. Leave it to her to make it more organized.

"Kristen's here," Macy announced, poking her head out of the door then quickly closing it behind her.

Mike took a steadying breath. Tonight was the night. He hoped.

3

———

*S*he knew Mike was going to be there, but pulling up and seeing his truck in the driveway solidified it and made it real. She really didn't want to deal with him tonight.

A long time ago she'd had it bad for Mike and his charming smile and smooth attitude, but he hadn't been interested in her. She wasn't upset about that and had pushed all those feelings down deep where they didn't bother her.

Mike was a player, everyone knew it. She knew it, and yet still she had to convince herself all over again when he singled her out. She hated it and loved it at the same time. Made her feel weak, but then lately what didn't?

Mike had slept with Laurel and jetted out before the sun. She didn't hold it against him, really. Laurel also slept around, but it hit home, and reminded her who he was at a time when she was letting her guard down around him and imagining a future.

She scoffed at herself. A future with Mike? How many women before her had imagined the same thing when he turned on all the charm? Pushing it from her mind, she steeled her spine and took a settling breath.

Grabbing her bag, she opened the car door and swung her legs out. With any luck she could start planning tonight on their couch instead of sitting around and wasting time she didn't have. Well, not wasting, but she could start a list of what she needed to do at least while talking to Macy.

Before she had stood up, Mike was at her car door waiting for her. Was she to have no peace?

"What, Mike?" she said by way of greeting.

"I brought you some flowers. I just wanted to give them to you before you got in the house in case you wanted to leave them in the car so you didn't forget them."

It was sweet, and then he used that grin that she'd seen charm many a woman before her and she reminded herself who he was. "Thanks." Taking the flowers, she resisted the urge to bury her face in them and take a deep breath, and placed them on the seat.

"I brought you some wine, too." Mike held out a glass she hadn't noticed he was carrying.

"Thank you." She took it, trying to balance her bag, keys, the glass, and her mind.

"Let me get that for you." Before she could say no, Mike had her bag off her shoulder with ease. He took her keys and shut the car door, hitting the lock on the remote. "Planning on working through dinner?"

"Maybe, I have a lot to do."

"I can feel that, it's no light bag, Kristen."

She watched as he looked down at her bag and noticed the book on top. She waited for the criticism to follow, or the jokes about it. He looked up, connecting his eyes with hers and holding her gaze.

"Good for you" was all he said and he held his arm out for her to lead the way into the house.

"Miss Parker!" Chris yelled as she came in. "Macy made me start my project already." He pouted as he wrapped her in a hug, nearly knocking the wine out of her glass.

"Did she?" Kristen bent over to whisper in his ear. "Just think of all the fun you'll be having Sunday when everyone else is trying to get theirs done."

Chris puzzled that one over and then smiled and took off again with his dog, Lucy, hot on his heels. Mike laughed behind her, and she stood up, straightening her back.

"Can you set my bag on the couch please?" she asked.

"Sure, need anything out of it first?" He held the bag out towards her.

"No, thank you."

"Kristen." One hand reached out and took hers. "I want to talk to you tonight, please?"

"There's nothing to say, Mike." She pulled her hand back, ignoring the heat that shot up her arm at his touch.

"On the contrary, I have a lot to say." He didn't reach for her hand again, but still she felt trapped.

Stalling to think of a response, she put the wine glass to her lips and drank until it was empty. "I think I need more." She spun on her heel to head toward the kitchen.

He let her go, didn't try to stop her again, but she heard him sigh and felt him follow her. It was just a few steps to the kitchen but Mike was right there to pour her glass for her. And again, to open the back door to where Daniel and Macy were.

"You made it!" Macy yelled.

"You didn't leave me much choice." Kristen muttered, earning a sheepish grin from Macy.

"Come, sit. The guys are cooking us dinner tonight." Macy patted the chair next to hers. "I've missed you; sorry I kinda forced you to come tonight."

"It's okay." It was an automatic response.

"It's not. I'm sorry; if you want to leave, I won't be mad." Macy looked concerned and a touch sad.

"It is okay. I might not stay long, as I said, but I am hungry." Winking she took another long sip of wine. It was going to be a long night.

She and Macy chatted about the baby and guessed at the gender. Macy was about halfway, she said, and was starting to show her baby bump through her clothes now. She was so happy to be an aunt and have a baby to love on.

"Feel," she said, grabbing Kristen's hand and putting it on her belly. "Do you feel that?"

Kristen nodded, lost for words. There was a slight flutter right there and there was something magical in feeling the life move inside of her.

She stood to get more wine, knowing she shouldn't be on her third glass already but not caring. Mike was in the kitchen, watching her, but not saying a word as she poured her glass. He waited for her to bring it to her lips before speaking.

"Have you eaten today?" he asked.

"What kind of question is that?"

"Just looking out for you is all."

"I can handle myself." Even as she said it, she wanted to take it back. Nothing like speaking those words into the universe to be proven wrong.

He walked to her and put one hand on her cheek, gently stroking it with the pad of his thumb. "I never said you couldn't."

She wouldn't have been able to fight him off had he tried anything right now. She expected him to lean in and kiss her but was left wanting instead. He dropped his hand and walked back outside with a plate of food in his hand.

She stood there not knowing how to feel or what to do. He had her in his hand right there, the perfect opportunity to say what it was he wanted or kiss her, and he walked away. Swirling her glass in her hand, she watched the liquid dance before settling down and going outside as well to eat.

They served themselves, steak, as usual, and Macy's homemade macaroni and cheese, with grilled corn. She contemplated switching her wine for a bottle of water instead, but decided she was feeling too good to do that. She'd be fine.

"Macy tells me you have the entire end-of-year show now?" Daniel asked.

"Yep. I just need to put it all together, find vendors, props, and everything else." Even she didn't know what everything else was now.

"What kind of props?" Mike asked.

"The entire set for the play, I guess." She took another sip. "My best guess is that nothing has been done and now it's on me to get it all pulled off."

"What's the play?" Macy asked.

Kristen laughed. "I have no idea." She hadn't gone through anything, and since she wasn't helping this year, she hadn't taken the time to learn. "I don't know if there is one." She laughed harder and then finished off her glass.

"I'll be back in a few weeks and can help you too, girl. You know we would all always take care of you, sport." David walked around her and ruffled her hair like he would a kid.

"Why do you do that?" Kristen groaned, as she always did.

The rest of dinner passed easily. No one questioned the play again and she was grateful for that. She grew more relaxed as the night passed.

She told Chris good night as he headed for bed and Macy and Daniel followed, leaving her outside with a very silent Mike, and a curious David.

"What?" she asked, finding him staring at her.

"I don't think I've ever seen you tipsy." He continued to stare at her.

"Stop staring," she said, throwing a napkin at him.

Mike laughed at her. "Relaxed looks good on you."

"Tonight only. I have things I should be doing right now instead of finishing off a bottle of wine."

"You do too much then if you don't have time to hang out with friends."

"Maybe." She was relaxed enough to confide in someone she knew she shouldn't. "I'm working on it."

"That's really good, Kristen. You'll be happier, I think."

"I'm going to read the room and head out." David stood to his full six feet and leveled a look at Mike. "Don't be stupid," he said, as he walked away.

Mike didn't acknowledge him. If he'd heard David, not a bit of it showed. Instead, his continued perusal of her was making her uncomfortable, so she tipped back her glass and finished that one too. He watched, and even when she closed her eyes, she knew he was still watching.

"What did you want to talk about then? Since it's just us and I'm too relaxed to fight with you."

"Not tonight."

For the second time today, she was left with her jaw on the ground. "Are you kidding?" He'd spent the better part of a year trying to talk to her and the moment she gives him the chance he passes?

"It's a serious conversation. It can wait."

"You're annoying, Mike," she told him, eliciting a deep laugh. It was a genuine laugh and the smile he gave her wasn't the practiced charming one, it was the better one, the one that was real and not meant to do anything to you. However, it was the one that did the most to her.

"Never did I think that not trying to talk to you was going to be the thing that annoyed you about me today."

"I'm out of wine." She pouted.

"I bought another bottle," he told her as he rose to go get it. Retuning quickly, he popped the cork and poured more in her glass.

"You bought all this wine for me?"

Mike nodded and set the bottle on the table.

"But now you don't want to talk to me because I drank it?" It didn't make sense to her.

"Apparently I didn't think everything through as well as I thought I did." Mike leaned back in his chair, still watching her, but more relaxed, as he stretched his long legs out in front of him.

"Nope. Not buying it. Just tell me what you want," she pressed.

"Why are you mad at me all the time, Kristen?"

"I'm not," she said, barely above a whisper.

"Explain."

"I'm not mad at you. I just don't want to be charmed. I'm not one of those women that you grin at, take home, and then forget about the next day."

Mike sat back up and looked at her for a long moment before speaking. "I never said you were."

"You didn't have to. One day you came in and started flashing that cheap grin at me and I'm not falling for it." She was being a little too honest tonight, but couldn't stop herself. "I don't like it and it's just so practiced." She made a face at him to show her disgust.

"That's it?"

Kristen nodded. "I liked you better before you started trying those moves on me."

He took a sip of his own beer and leaned back again. "You're a mystery."

"I'm not."

The conversation ended as Daniel and Macy returned with a deck of cards. They played spades and talked, laughing as the time passed. She nearly finished the second bottle of wine before she couldn't wait any longer and stood to find the bathroom.

Unfortunately, she hadn't stood in a while and in that time had drank what amounted to a bottle and a half of wine. The alcohol hit her suddenly, causing her to topple. She would have fallen had Mike not jumped up to catch her.

"I'm okay," she told him, trying to shrug him off.

"Sure," he soothed, making her want to do it on her own even more.

"Just let me help you to the door," he said.

"I've gotta get home," she told him. "It's late."

"It is late, but I think you're staying here tonight."

"Can't, too much to do," she told him.

"Guys, I'm taking Kristen home," he announced, and pulled her into the house.

"I can get myself home."

"Not tonight." He stopped them near the bathroom door and let go of her, making sure she had her balance before backing away. "I'll get you home tonight."

She didn't want to fight with him, so she went into the bathroom and closed the door. She did what she needed to do and then splashed some water on her face. Damn, he was right, she couldn't drive. Resigned, she went in search of her ride.

4

Kristen had her bag in her lap, hugging it tightly, and was sound asleep in the front seat of his truck. She fell asleep within a few minutes of leaving and her house was only about fifteen minutes away.

They were parked in her driveway as he contemplated the best way to get her into the house. Deciding to carry her in, he got out and went around to the passenger side to look for her keys. He ran and unlocked the door, setting her bag inside and leaving the door open so he didn't have to fumble with the knob while carrying her.

Getting her out of the car and into his arms was easier than he thought it would be. She didn't squirm, rather nuzzled into his chest, and he stood there for a moment and let her get adjusted, savoring the moment before carrying her in.

It was only after he made it into the house that he realized he had no idea where her room was other than upstairs. Short of checking all the doors, which, frankly, would have made him feel like a creeper, he laid her down on the couch.

She whimpered when he moved away, and reached out for him. "I'm just taking your shoes off." He laughed at her and slid her shoes off both feet. Taking the blanket off the back of the couch, he laid it across her, preparing to walk out the door.

"You're warm," Kristen said.

"Go back to sleep," he told her.

"Can't. I'm cold." She never opened her eyes and Mike wondered if she was truly awake or not.

"If you want to walk, I'll help you to your room so you can get in bed," He waited by the door for her to make up her mind.

"No. You come here," she told him.

It was wrong. He should have left. There was no way she really knew what she was saying, but he did it anyway.

He sat on the couch near her head and put a pillow on his lap, helping her onto it. She squirmed and got comfortable before relaxing again.

He reached for the remote laying neatly on the side table and settled in for the night. After finding some TV show he could watch without paying much attention, he gently lowered his hand to her hair, trying not to wake her.

He played with her hair and told himself over and over that he would leave shortly, as soon as he was sure that moving her wouldn't wake her up. No clue when that might be, or if he would really leave.

He wasn't aware he'd dozed off until he felt her move and then heard her cuss.

"Shit." She sat all the way up as he opened his eyes. "Oh, really shit." Grabbing her head, she bent over her knees.

"I'll get you some medicine." He stood, ignoring her complaints, and headed for the kitchen.

He got a glass of water, but after checking all the cabinets, didn't find any medicine. "Where would I find medicine?" he yelled from the kitchen.

She groaned as he walked in the living room and set the water down. She mumbled something about bathroom and he walked down the hall in search of it. Luckily it was the second door he opened, after an office.

He dumped a few in his hand and put the bottle back where he found it, admiring the simple and surprising decor of everything. He had expected pink and flowers, instead finding a beach-themed bathroom and no flowers or frills in sight.

Handing her the pills, she swallowed them down with a gulp of water and thanked him.

"Finish the water too; you're going to need it."

"I know how to handle a hangover, Mike," she half whispered.

"I'll make you some breakfast."

"Please, don't."

"Go shower. You'll feel better." Not waiting for an answer, he left her on the couch and walked towards the kitchen.

A pillow hit him square in the back and he smiled. She hadn't tossed him out, so he'd take a pillow to his back during her hangover as a win.

She had more breakfast food than he'd expected and he was having a hard time reconciling the home he was in with the Kristen that he knew. Again, he'd expected something more girly, maybe some smoothie stuff, and instead there was bacon, sausage, and eggs in the fridge.

He hummed as he made a decent breakfast for both of them, laughing only a little when he heard the shower cut off. She was probably mad at him for suggesting it and then herself for doing as he suggested.

"I hate to say it but it smells delicious in here."

"I know you do. Eat up." Setting a plate in front of her, she dug in right away. "I didn't know how you liked your eggs so I went with scrambled."

"Scrambled is my preference." After a long drink of water, she continued, "As much as I appreciate breakfast, why are you here?"

"You asked me to stay."

"I did not."

"You definitely did."

He watched her face as she thought back to last night and knew the moment that memory trickled in.

"Oh my God." Her face turned red and he watched as the color floated down her cheeks, her neck, and wondered how far it went. "I don't know what to say."

"Say thank you, for breakfast."

"Thank you." She took another bite and had nearly finished her plate when someone knocked on the door. "Excuse me." She stood and went for the door. He couldn't see her as he started to clean up his mess from cooking, but he could barely hear her.

"We saw Mike's truck in the driveway and just had to stop and say hi. He never comes to town anymore."

Mike put on his most charming smile and turned to greet three old women that were too nosy for their own good. The Pillars is what they were called collectively. He'd be damned if he couldn't remember their names right now, but he'd fake it unless they called him out.

"Turns out you have company," Kristen joined them all in the kitchen, "at my house."

"I didn't invite them," he whispered to her as she came closer.

"It's so nice to see you two finally together," the one in blue said.

"We're not—"Kristen tried.

"You cook?" the one in red said.

"Oh, and look, he cleans up too!" the last lady in green said. "Isn't that sweet?"

"I am just—"Mike tried.

"Nonsense," the one in red cut him off.

"Well, we will get going." The one in green ushered her friends out.

"We expect to see more of you," the one in blue said, and with the same whir of activity, they left.

Mike and Kristen were left standing in the kitchen staring at the empty entryway.

"What just happened?" Mike asked.

"We've been managed." Kristen groaned. "The whole town will think you slept here last night."

"I did sleep here last night."

"You know what I mean."

"We could make sure they aren't telling a lie?"

"Don't start. This is not how I planned my weekend."

"Well, I'm about to change things a bit for you too, because now that you're sober, I'd really like to talk to you."

Kristen started to say something and then sighed and plopped down in the chair. "I'm too tired to fight you."

"Encouraging."

"Don't be a smart-ass."

"Wouldn't dream of it." He joined her at the other side of the table so he could look at her as he talked. "I want to clear the air between us. I know you said some things last night, but I want to have a serious conversation."

"It's not that big of a deal, Mike."

"It is if you won't even talk to me or stay in the same room around me." He waited for her to argue and when she didn't, he continued. "I want to understand what happened, what led you to be so mad at me."

"Ugh!" She rubbed her head. "It's not that simple."

"Well, start by explaining what you said last night."

She stared at him for a moment. "Fine." Taking a deep breath, she let it out before she started. "Look, it's a few things, and I'm not sure it will even make sense to you."

"I'm going to try to understand," he said honestly.

"It was after you went out with my friend."

"I didn't go out with her."

She held up a hand. "Just let me talk. You took her home, and then left her there."

"Nothing happened," he said in defense.

She gave him a look with one raised eyebrow, that no doubt was practiced and meant for second graders that said be quiet, but silently scolded.

"After that happened, I started to look at you a little differently." She paused and looked him in the eye. "It's your smile."

"That's what you said last night."

"It's practiced charm and I didn't like it being used on me. Like you were trying to get something from me and it started to make me feel cheap."

He opened his mouth to speak but stopped, waiting instead to see what she said next. She was right, he didn't get it.

"You do this on all women to get what you want, and it works. I'm not even mad that it works for you, but I'm mad that it started to work on me and I didn't even notice at first. Then it made me feel like another one of your women, Mike, and there are plenty of them."

Processing that took an awkward moment before he could respond. "Two things."

"Oh wait, let me add, sorry, I did finally find out the truth about that night. She came clean and, you wouldn't know, but we don't talk much anymore. I don't do liars."

"Fair. One thing, then. I want to understand. You're saying you don't want to talk to me because I smile at you like I do other women?"

"If you have to break it down like that, yeah." She had just a hint of sarcasm in her tone.

"I don't get it." He was more confused than he was before.

"I told you."

"I know, but what about that makes you not talk to me?"

"Honestly?"

"Please."

"It was starting to work on me. I felt it when you gave me that charm, and it worried me to know it was the same charm you used on all the women. You just did it today to Ethel."

He had. "So, to get it straight, you were starting to fall for me a little? And then you thought about it and felt," he trailed off, looking for a word to use.

"Cheap." She filled in for him.

"Okay, follow-up question." He shouldn't ask it, but he was going to anyway. "What, then, would work?"

"Seriously?"

"Very."

"Nothing Mike. I don't think we should go there at all."

"I want to, you want to, we're adults, what's wrong with trying?"

"It's not a good idea."

"Why? Because you decided?"

"Mike." Kristen held his gaze again. "Look at me, I am so far from the women you are usually with. Why would you even want to?"

"Maybe I am looking for something different. Maybe I'm just interested in you."

"Maybe, I don't fully trust you."

That left him stunned. Trust him? She had no reason not to. "What the hell is that supposed to mean?"

"It means what I said. I don't know if I can trust you. I'm not a fling kind of person and you are. We are just really different, and I don't know that I wouldn't be waiting for you to get bored of the relationship thing."

"Wow."

"You asked for honest."

"Yeah, I did." He thought on it, and decided he needed more time to think on it. "I need to know we can talk. I'm still going to try, I won't lie, but I'll do my best to show you I want something different."

"Mike—"

"Let's talk about something else. What's the new project at work? A play?"

"Yes?" The question was there like she didn't quite know if she wanted the subject changed.

"How can I help?"

"As much as I would like to say you don't have to, I actually could use some help with props."

She spent the next hour going over the notes she had in the binder, her learning about things as she discussed it with him. They had moved from the kitchen table to the living room with Mike on the couch and her on the floor looking things over.

The play, it seemed, was about woodland creatures learning not to be shy. Cute for elementary kids, but sounded like a lot of work.

Kristen had explained her coworker and Beth's straight dislike of Kristen, something he didn't get anymore than she did. Kristen was nice to everyone, all the time. Even when she didn't want to be near him, she was never mean, just avoided him.

"So, you need a set. Trees, forest, et cetera?"

"Yeah, it seems like it."

"What's the size of the stage and the height you need?"

"I have no idea."

"Monday afternoon then?"

"Huh?"

"I'll come by the school and meet you there to take some measurements."

"We can't pay you for this. No fundraising was done."

"Charitable donation for me then."

She stared at him, "you're serious? You're going to help?"

"Sure."

"Thank you, so much. You have no idea how much this really does help."

"Help is my middle name."

She laughed at him. "Sure, it is."

"All right, I will get out of your hair. Do you want a ride back to Daniel's for your car?"

"No, I think maybe I'll get more done if no one thinks I'm home."

"Probably true. I'll see you after school on Monday?"

"Call me when you get there and I will come meet you and show you around."

5

____

The school day seemed to both drag on and fly by at the same time. As she walked her class out to the busses, she wondered if Mike was there yet. She told herself it was just because she didn't want him to wait too long since he was doing her a favor. It definitely wasn't because she wanted to see him.

She didn't need the drama of Mike in her life, always trying to charm his way out of something, or into something. It wasn't going to work on her, she reminded herself.

Just as the last bus drove off, she got a text from Mike saying he was here. She told him to meet her by the front doors and quickly walked through the school to meet him. The bus parking lot was at the back of the school to reduce traffic with the parents, and she was stopped no less than three times as she headed to meet him.

He had been kept company while waiting though, she noticed as she approached, and she saw him talking to Beth. She almost walked away and left him there, but straightened her back a little and held her head high as she approached.

"Hey, Kristen." Mike greeted her with a wave. "Beth was just telling me about the play."

"I bet she was." Kristen said to him but looked at Beth instead.

Beth smiled sweetly and nodded. "It seems Mike here is going to help and I was just thinking that I might be able to free up a little time on my schedule to help out."

She wanted to stomp her feet again. At this point she should just start doing it, it couldn't be good to hold it in all the time, all this frustration.

"Kristen was just going to show me around a bit," Mike said and moved to Kristen's side.

"I can do that, I'm sure she has plenty to do," Beth answered.

"Actually, this is what I need to do." Kristen took Mike's hand to pull him along and away from Beth. "If you'll excuse us."

"I think I'll join you two. I'd love to hear how things are coming along, with it only a month away." Beth walked to Mike's other side, creating a sandwich of him between them.

"It's okay," Mike whispered and squeezed her hand.

The tour of the auditorium hadn't gone as she had hoped. Mike made measurements as Beth attempted small talk and Kristen stood off to the side. It was awkward, and she hated that it was her left in the background but didn't know how to get out of it.

"I think I have what I need," Mike said, closing his tablet cover.

"Let me walk you out," Beth said and practically hung on one arm.

"I have some things to discuss with Kristen first. Thanks for joining us though."

"About the play? I'd love to hear your thoughts."

"This is more of a personal nature," he told her.

"Oh well, I can wait for a few minutes. We can't really have personal guests on school property."

She couldn't help it: the eye roll was the perfect response to the way that Beth was behaving. Mike saw her and barely stifled a laugh.

It was time she jumped into the conversation, if she was to have any chance of talking to Mike today.

"Let me get my bag, Mike, and we can leave together. Would you like to walk with me to my class, so you can kind of get a feel for the kids?" She put her best shot out there.

"Or I can walk you out while Kristen gets her bag," Beth offered.

Mike declined and walked with Kristen instead. He waited until they got to her classroom before he spoke.

"That's her, huh?"

"Yeah." She couldn't hide the sadness it gave her to have had that whole exchange even happen and then to have Mike notice it. It was worse that a high school bully somedays.

"Rest assured I have zero interest in her."

"You can do what you want, Mike."

"Can I?" he asked.

She nodded, not looking up. Putting several things in her bag to work on for the night, she didn't notice when Mike rounded the desk. Didn't notice how close he was until his hand was on her chin urging her to look up at him.

"I want to kiss you," he said deeply.

"We—we can't here." It was the only defense she had from him right now, because in this moment, she wanted nothing more than for him to kiss her.

"Fair enough." Mike backed away. "But I notice you didn't say no."

"Mike—"

"Kristen!" Principal Jenkins came into the room. "Beth was telling me that you found someone to help with the set and I wanted to come meet him."

She looked to the ceiling and hoped for patience because this day was testing every bit of it. "This is Mike; he's agreed to donate his time to help us build a set."

The men shook hands and greeted each other as Beth joined them in her room. Kristen sat back down in her chair with a sigh, would she never leave?

"Oh good, you found him," she said to Jenkins.

"I did. It was very nice to meet you, thank you for helping our school out on such short notice."

"It's no problem, just helping out a friend," Mike said.

"Thank you just the same." Jenkins turned towards Kristen. "If you need anything just let me know, glad to see the progress you're making."

"Thanks."

She was watching Beth try to get close to Mike again. Annoying was the best way to describe her at this moment, or maybe all moments.

"Kristen, are you ready to head out?" Mike asked.

"Yeah, just let me—" She was going to say she needed to get her bag, but Mike was there getting it for her.

"Let's head out," he said. "Nice meeting everyone."

They could hear Beth's heels behind them as they left the school. She never turned to look at her until they reached Kristen's car. When she turned, she found her standing there at the entrance, watching them.

"She really doesn't like you," Mike said.

"She really does like you," Kristen added.

"Do you trust me?"

"What?"

"I wanna do something, do you trust me?"

"Yes?" Whatever it was, it definitely wasn't going to be a good idea.

"Is she still watching?" he asked.

Kristen peeked around Mike and nodded.

"Good. Let's give her a show."

Mike moved around her so swiftly she barely noticed, and made it so their profiles were facing the school: anyone at the front door could see both of them.

This time when he cupped her chin, he lowered his mouth to hers without asking. She'd told him she trusted him and supposed this was what she got for doing so.

As soon as his lips touched hers, she felt electricity from her lips to her toes. When his tongue touched her lips, she opened for him and felt her knees go weak. Mike's hand left her chin and slid to the back of her neck, the other arm snaking around her waist, giving her the support she needed.

She kissed him back. It had been a while since she'd kissed

anyone, but she did it anyway, without thinking of all her fears about where they were, if she was good enough, if she was too rusty at it.

The kiss matched the day in that it seemed to last forever and not long enough at the same time. When Mike pulled away, he rested his forehead on hers as they both caught their breath.

"Next time, there won't be an audience," he promised. "I'll meet you at your place if that's okay? To go over the set?"

She just nodded. There were no words, and she wasn't sure she was in any shape to drive yet. He helped her into her car and shut the door before walking around to climb into his truck.

A few deep breaths helped clear a little of the fog from her brain and she put the car in gear. She was almost to her house before she thought of Beth and hoped that no one else saw them in the parking lot. She did let herself smile, thinking of what Beth's reaction must have been to seeing them.

Mike pulled up behind her car and was getting her bag out of the backseat before she could even get out.

"I can get it," she told him.

"Surprisingly, it has to weigh as much as you."

Instead of replying, she unlocked the door and let them in the house.

"Living room or kitchen?" he asked.

"Living room, please."

"Do you have to carry so much back and forth?" he asked.

Shrugging, she pulled out the binder for the play and opened it on the table, followed by her laptop. Mike laid his tablet on his lap and pulled out a stylus.

"Give me just a few minutes, I want to show you what I am thinking."

She nodded and tried to focus on the papers in front of her, but couldn't help but watch him as he slid the stylus around on the screen. It was mesmerizing to watch him draw, something that she'd never seen him do.

Sure, she'd seen some of his sketches, but she'd never watched him work. He concentrated harder than she'd ever seen him and there was something about his focus that begged to be observed.

"Here." He turned the tablet around and handed it to her as he finished.

She was more than impressed as she looked at what he'd put together. There was a rough outline of the stage, including the curtains, and he had drawn a large tree in the middle and a few clusters of trees throughout the rest of the stage.

"These would be mostly in the back, but we can put them on casters so they can be moved around and if you need to have the kids hide behind them or something, that could be done."

"Mike...." She had no words.

"If you don't like it, that's okay. I can come up with something else if you let me know what you want."

He was nervous? That was something she never thought she'd see.

"I love it. You captured exactly what I needed." She looked at it again and then back at him. "Are you sure you can do it before the play?"

"I'd need to start right away, but yeah, I can get it done."

"Thank you, really." She handed him back his tablet.

"Where should I build them at?"

"What do you mean?"

"I can do them at my house, but I am worried about transporting them here, as big as they need to be. I'd like to build them at the school, if I can?"

"I'd have to get permission, but I don't see why not. Probably only after school though."

"Okay, let me know and we will come up with a plan." He closed the cover back on the tablet. "Do you want me to paint them too?"

"If you can that would be great."

He nodded. "I was thinking once you know who is going to be in the play, we can put apples on the big tree, and maybe use kids' handprints instead of painting real apples?"

It was so thoughtful she was shocked it came from him. It seemed she had a lot to learn about Mike.

"I think that would be great, they'd love it and I think the parents would too."

"It's settled then, just let me know when and where I can get started. If I can't do it at the school, I'll reach out to Daniel. Text me?"

"Okay."

With that, Mike left her sitting there stunned. He was so thoughtful that she didn't know how to fit the man that just left her house with the one that she thought she knew. He hadn't even mentioned the kiss or tried again. That was bothering her more than it should.

Pushing it from her mind, she worked on her next line of business and started going through kids that would be chosen for the show. She'd get to see Mike again soon, and until then she wasn't going to stress over him, or the kiss.

6

$\mathcal{K}$risten had immediately gone to get permission for Mike to work on-site when she got to school the next morning.

Once she had the go ahead, she texted Mike who told her he would be by Friday afternoon to pick her up to get supplies and dinner. She'd tried texting him back after that to get clarity on what he meant, but he never responded. He was trapping her into the plans, but she didn't mind, just wanted to know where they were going.

She was still smiling when Beth walked into her classroom about five minutes before the kids were going to.

"Well, you seem to be in a good mood," Beth commented,

"I am, thanks for noticing," Kristen replied. She wasn't going to let Beth ruin her day.

"I recognize your little boy toy from somewhere. Any ideas?"

"No. You'd have to ask him," she answered as casually as she could, despite her thoughts trying to decide where Beth might know him from.

"Well, it wouldn't be anywhere he'd been with you for sure." Beth did her normal spin on one heel and left the room.

What was that supposed to mean, Kristen wondered. She didn't get to think on it much before kids started to join her in the classroom. Pushing all of it to the back of her mind, she greeted her students and began her day.

She managed to keep the thoughts at bay until she had time for lunch, where she finally had time to think. Pulling out her phone she debated texting Mike to see if he knew Beth from anywhere, but decided against it. If he'd remembered her from anywhere, he'd have mentioned it.

Instead, she texted Macy to ask how they were doing and to try to take her mind off Mike. Unfortunately, that plan backfired.

Everyone's doing good here, you?

Doing good. Getting some stuff done for the play. Is it okay if Chris gets a part?

Of course it's okay!

Consider him in then. :)

How are things going with Mike?

What do you mean?

You know it's all over town that y'all are sleeping together?

OMG!

Your brother is fit to be tied.

I haven't slept with Mike.

Not what the Pillars are telling everyone.

You've got to be freaking kidding me.

Nope. Call me tonight and tell me what's going on?

... I can't. I have plans.

You have plans? What plans?

Umm.

OMG it's with Mike, isn't it?

Shut up.

Call me after. I'll stay up.

I'll try.

Putting her phone back in her drawer, she quickly took a few more bites of the salad she had packed as kids began returning to class. The rest of the day she was more distracted than she would have liked.

At the end of the day, she walked the kids out to their buses and quickly dipped back into the classroom to grab her things, hoping to avoid Beth. Luck wasn't on her side as she ran into Beth in the hall as she was leaving.

"I haven't figured it out yet, have you?" Beth asked.

"Figured out what?" How to frustrate me more? she added in her head.

"Don't play dumb, it doesn't work for you."

"Whatever." Kristen started to walk away again.

"I am talking about the man you were kissing in the parking lot. What's his name?"

She didn't stop walking. Wasn't sure what Beth was trying to do, but she wasn't sticking around for it today. Beth's heels clicked on the floor behind her, though. She wasn't going to get away easy it seemed.

"Mike. That's it." Click, click, click on the floor and her nerves. "I'm certain I have met him somewhere before."

"Beth, I don't care. Ask him yourself. I have stuff to get done."

"Fine, be rude. I'll ask him now."

Kristen looked up at the sky and prayed for patience. She was at the end of her rope today and Beth was making sure she started to lose her grip on it.

"Oh, Mike!" Beth waved at him as they crossed the parking lot.

Mike looked confused but threw up one hand in greeting. He was just being polite of course, she told herself. Kristen didn't wave, sure he had been responding to Beth and not greeting her. She didn't speak when they approached him either, waiting for Beth to get her nonsense out of the way.

"I just know, I know you from somewhere. Any ideas?" Beth asked Mike.

"Let me get your stuff, Kristen." Mike ignored Beth and took her bag.

"Thanks," she muttered.

"I think it was a party or something. I'm trying so hard to remember," Beth whined.

"Can't say I know you from anywhere," Mike told her before turning to Kristen. "Ready to go, babe?" he asked her.

Kristen just nodded. Babe? He had to be putting on another show for Beth, she reminded herself before she took his hand for him to help her in the truck. There was no graceful way to climb up into the truck for someone that wasn't used to literally having to pull themselves up into it.

"I missed you," he said loud enough for Beth to hear, then kissed her on the lips.

It wasn't the deep kiss it had been yesterday, just a peck, a show of affection for the audience. He helped her into his truck and walked around the other side with Beth hot on his heels.

"Have a good night," he said as he hopped in the truck and practically shut the door in her face. "What is her problem?"

"I don't know. She's been asking me if I knew how she knows you since before school started this morning."

"What the hell is wrong with her?"

She shrugged and turned to look out the window as he drove.

"Wanna listen to some music or something?" he asked.

"I'm good. You can put on whatever."

"What's wrong?"

"Nothing."

"You're not acting like nothing."

"It's just been a long day and Beth didn't help."

"I can imagine she can dampen anyone's good mood. Screw her."

Kristen smiled, but even she knew it was a sad smile. She was having to remind herself too much today that the affection he was showing to her was to make Beth jealous of Kristen and nothing more.

Problem was, if she didn't remind herself, she'd forget, and it was entirely too easy to forget. Mike had said he wanted them to be able to talk again, and she wasn't having a problem with it, but she wasn't having it easy either.

Every time he looked at her, she felt butterflies like a damn teenager and it was driving her mad. She wanted him to kiss her and mean it. She wanted more than that, but she wasn't going to say that.

"Kristen, just tell me what's wrong," he said as they got off the highway near the home improvement store.

"Nothing is wrong, I'm fine."

"Fine."

Now he was mad, and she knew there was going to be no good day ahead of her now. The day had started out nice enough, she'd been happy until she remembered it was all for show. Now she was more irritated at herself than anyone or anything else.

They parked and she waited for Mike to come around and open her door for her. She could have done it herself but he probably would have been irritated at her for that too, so she waited.

When she turned to get out of the truck though, she was face-to-face with Mike.

"Please tell me what's wrong."

"I've just had a day is all."

"What happened?" he prodded.

"Why?"

He looked like someone just kicked his puppy. Somewhere between anger and hurt.

"I thought we were getting somewhere with each other and you won't even tell me why you're having a bad day?"

"Mike...."

She didn't get to finish as he backed away and helped her out of the truck. She didn't try again, just followed him through the store and pointed out different paint colors when he asked for her opinion.

They weren't rude to each other, just both very quiet. Saying the right things at the right time, but nothing more, nothing less. She hated it.

As they loaded up the truck, Kristen chewed on her bottom lip. She'd have to be the one to say something since she'd gone and ruined the friendship they were building.

He, once again, helped her into the truck and walked around to climb in.

"Mike," she said as he shut his door.

"What?"

"I'm sorry."

"For what?" he asked.

"For being in a mood today. I've got a lot on my mind and you kissing me to make Beth jealous doesn't help clear my mind."

"What?" he smacked the steering wheel. "Kristen. I want to kiss you and she has nothing to do with it."

"Yesterday—"

"Sure, it was a bonus that she was watching, it let her know I wasn't interested in her." He faced her and reached out for one of her hands. "I kissed you because I wanted to. The timing was just a plus."

She struggled to make it all make sense as Mike raised one hand to her mouth and touched his thumb to her bottom lip.

"Stop chewing, you'll make it bleed," he said quietly.

He leaned over and kissed her bottom lip.

"Mike."

"Kristen."

"I don't know how to do this. Us."

"You don't have to. We will figure it out as we go."

She buckled her seatbelt still in a daze as Mike did the same and started driving. He headed back towards her house, but his hand slipped over her knee as he drove. He didn't try anything and didn't even move when he did it, but the electricity practically radiated through her at the touch.

"Can we drop this stuff at the school before dinner?"

"Sure," she answered after clearing her throat.

"Do you want me to move my hand? I don't want to make you uncomfortable; all you have to do is tell me and I'll stop anything."

She didn't trust her voice so she shook her head instead. It wasn't uncomfortable in a bad way. It was making her a little anxious, but also a little excited, and while she wasn't sure what she was going to do with that energy, she didn't want to let it go either.

Thankfully when they made it to school Beth's car was gone. They quickly unloaded the paints and materials into the auditorium side door. The custodian helped and then locked the door behind them.

"Grab your car and I'll follow you to your place so it's not left here." Mike kissed her sweetly again and waited for her to drive off before following her home.

She parked her car and Mike got her bag out of his truck. "Want to put this inside before we go?"

"Sure." She unlocked the door to the house and Mike followed her in. "On second thought, you wanna eat in tonight?"

"I'd love that," he said as he dropped her bag on the floor.

In two long strides Mike was touching her. He pressed his hands to her hair as she tilted her head back, ready for his kiss. He didn't disappoint either.

In one movement, he had her back against the wall and his mouth on hers. His tongue warred with hers as she moaned against him. One hand left her hair and slid down her back causing a shiver to follow.

He pulled back from her mouth to trail kisses down her cheek to her neck. She didn't try to stifle her small sounds of pleasure. This was heaven and she was going to savor every bit of it with her hands clutching his shoulders.

"Kristen," he practically growled as he backed away. "You're going to be the death of me."

They were both panting and her brain was in a fog. Her legs were barely supporting her and she was scared that if she let go of him, she'd melt into the floor.

"Come on, let's go see what's in your fridge."

He backed away slowly, giving her a chance to get her bearings before she let go of his shirt.

"Sorry," she whispered.

"For what?"

"Umm, for not letting go."

Mike bent down and hooked one arm behind her knees and the other behind her back, picking her up and taking her to the kitchen.

"Don't apologize for holding on to me." He kissed her again as he set her on the kitchen counter. "Now, let's find food before this night goes further than we want it to."

She laughed and jumped off the counter. He was right, but if he'd carried her to the bedroom instead of the kitchen she wouldn't have complained.

"Steaks?" she asked, pulling two out of the fridge.

"You have steak in your fridge?" he asked.

"I thought you might come by, and if you didn't, I was going to have a very good lunch for the rest of the week," she admitted.

"Dammit," Mike said, pulling out his phone.

Kristen glanced over to see "Elizabeth" on the screen and then backed away. It didn't mean anything, she told herself. He answered the phone and walked into the living room as she started prepping the steaks with seasoning to get them out on the grill.

Mike was always the one to cook at Daniel's when they were all there, but she knew her way around a grill too. In short order she had the grill started and was back inside rummaging her fridge for sides.

He was still on the phone when she poked her head into the living room to ask if he wanted corn or a salad.

"Look, I'm sorry, I didn't know." He ran a hand through his hair, and then let it drop to his side.

She watched and waited for his attention for a moment before turning and trying to forget what she'd heard. She didn't make it far before Mike spoke again.

"I know." He sighed. "I know what you wanted, but that wasn't going to happen. I told you that then, and I am telling you again now, I'm not going to marry you."

Freezing in place, she dropped the corn on the floor as she leaned against the wall for support. Mike ran right into her in the hallway, practically knocking her over.

"I, uh, wanted to know what side you wanted," she stammered, picking the corn up.

She didn't look at him, just headed back to the kitchen trying to make sense of what she'd heard and wondering if it was something she could even ask him about.

"Kristen?" Mike started. "I think we need to talk."

"Later? The grill is hot," she said, avoiding him and carrying the steaks out to the deck.

It was clear that whatever he wanted to say wasn't going to be good, and she didn't want to hear it yet. She just needed a moment to brace herself.

7

Mike stood in Kristen's kitchen trying to figure out how he was going to tell her that he definitely did know Beth, even if he'd forgotten. Well, technically he knew Elizabeth and it had been years since he'd seen her. She was a lot different now.

When he'd known her, she'd gone by her full name and had brown hair. She'd not dressed like she'd been when he'd seen her at the school. She wore jean shorts and crop tops and had hung with his friends at the bar when he'd gotten back from his first tour of duty.

Their mothers had been friends, it turned out, and they were more than excited to see their kids hanging out. He'd spent two weeks staying with his mother and mostly drunk, hanging out with Beth almost every night.

Then he'd gone back to the army and not given her another thought. He'd not promised her anything, but she'd called often until she finally got the hint that he wasn't going to answer. After the calls stopped, he'd simply forgotten about it.

He'd had the same thought that she seemed familiar, but brushed it off as just being a hot chick that he might had flirted with one time. Apparently, he'd done more than that, and now he needed to break it to Kristen that her work nemesis was a former fling, and he didn't think it was going to go well.

He made himself busy and carried the corn out to her, deciding he'd wait until they sat down to eat. She'd clearly heard something before he'd hung up on Beth, but he didn't know exactly what. She wasn't the type to snoop, he didn't think, so he'd guessed it wasn't a lot, but it was enough to make her run from him again.

Also, Beth had known what she was doing by telling Kristen she'd known him from somewhere but not where. She'd played her little game, something that she'd been good at even back when he'd known her, and it worked. She had got her doubts all over Kristen and he wasn't sure how he'd fix it.

Kristen had finished cooking while he got plates out and set the table. She wasn't looking at him and didn't speak as she plated the food and took her seat.

"I'm sorry," he began.

She picked up her fork and then set it back down again and put her hands in her lap. Looking at him, she waited for him to continue.

"Turns out I do know Beth." Best to just go ahead and get it out of the way.

Kristen blew out a breath but didn't speak.

"It was a long time ago, after our first deployment, and I came home for a few weeks."

Kristen pushed her chair back and started to get up. "Okay." Abandoning him at the table, she grabbed a beer from the fridge and leaned against the counter.

"I swear to you, I didn't recognize her, she looked nothing like she does now."

"She knew who you were though, didn't she?"

Mike nodded. "I think so. Kristen, please, I really didn't know."

"Who, what, was she to you?" she asked calmly.

"We slept together if that's what you're asking."

He watched as she processed that information. Saw her shoulders fall as she studied the label on her bottle of beer and picked at it with her nails.

"I don't know what to do with that information," she told him.

"I don't either." He wanted to go to her but stayed in his seat for fear she'd run away, or worse, reject him outright. "It doesn't change anything between us. Everything that's happened over the last few days."

"Doesn't it though?"

Now he did get up and go to her, pulling her in for a hug and breathing a small sigh of relief when she let him. "It doesn't. She's in my past and you're my present and my future. She doesn't matter."

"She matters some,. You still had her name in your phone from years ago."

"I'll delete it, right now." He reached for his phone in his pocket.

"No, that's not what I want you to do. I'm just saying, you still had her there, so she must mean or did mean something to you."

"More like I never delete anything from my phone. My parent's old landline is still in there too. I just don't go through my phone."

Kristen nodded against his shoulder and backed away. "I can't guarantee anything, Mike, but I'm going to try to put this out of my mind. It's just, why her? Why'd it have to be her?"

He knew what she meant, and honestly, he had the same thoughts, but there was nothing he could do about it now except try to move forward with Kristen. They returned to the table and ate in an almost comfortable silence, a far cry from the mood they'd been in a short while ago.

"What did she want?" Kristen asked.

"To yell at me for not knowing who she was and for not calling her back years ago," he answered honestly.

Kristen laughed. "Well, can confirm it's the same person."

"Oh, without a doubt." He laughed as well.

"My brother thinks we're sleeping together," she blurted.

Beer came out his mouth and nose as he choked on that statement. "What?"

"Macy told me the whole town has been informed by the Pillars." She took a long sip of her own beer and handed him a napkin. "I told her we weren't, but I don't know how that's going to go over."

He blew out a breath and cleared his throat as he cleaned up the mess he'd just made. "He was going to find out eventually."

"Yeah."

"How do you feel about it?" he asked cautiously.

"I'm less concerned with Daniel than I am the whole town in general." She started clearing their plates as she continued, "But I don't know how I feel about it, when we aren't even actually sleeping together."

"We can rectify that tonight," he joked.

"Very funny."

He helped her clean up as they both processed the day and the news. It was a lot to take in and he wasn't looking forward to the conversation with Daniel.

"I have to get some work done." Sitting in the floor with her bag, she spread her papers all over the coffee table.

"I have some things I can work on as well if you don't mind my hanging out for a little longer?" he asked, not in a hurry to leave her.

"Go ahead, though I'm not good company when I'm busy, I'm afraid."

"It's okay, me either."

He went to his truck and grabbed his tablet. He really did have some work he needed to get done and some bids he needed to go over. Sitting here with her was just easier somehow. They weren't talking or even looking at each other, both heads buried in their own work, but it was just nice to be near her.

Kristen stood and stretched. "You want something to drink?"

"I could use a break to be honest." He stood and followed her into the kitchen.

They each grabbed a drink and Kristen grabbed a bowl of grapes from the fridge and led him outside. The deck wasn't huge, but there was a small table outside and four chairs. She rarely entertained at her own house. Usually, evenings were at Daniel's, or she would get talked into attending someone else's get-together.

Seeing Mike at the table now was almost comical. She had bought the small wrought iron set years ago, but it wasn't meant for tall men to sit at. It perfectly fit her small frame. He didn't complain though, only adjusted himself a few times before kicking his legs out to accommodate himself.

"You sure you want to sit out here?" she asked him.

"I'm fine; I don't think I'll break anything." He winked at her.

The sound of crickets filled the air. An owl hooted somewhere in the distance, and Kristen wasn't sure if the silence was as awkward for him as it was for her, so hesitated to break it.

"Tell me something," Mike broke the silence first, "that no one else knows."

"Umm. That's a little personal, don't you think?"

He simply shrugged and watched her. She tried not to shift under his gaze and to think of something to say.

"I hate not being able to tell people no," she finally said.

"I know that about you already," he told her. "But, since I think that was an admission on your part, I'll accept it. Your turn to ask a question."

"Are we playing a game now?"

"Is that your question?"

Kristen shook her head and thought about what she could ask him. "Tell me about your family."

"What a waste of a question."

"It's my question, I get to decide if it's wasteful or not."

"Your loss." Mike took a sip of his drink before speaking again. "There's nothing to say really. I don't have any siblings. My dad left a long time ago and I don't know him at all. My mom is a serial bride. She loves to get married and is on her fifth, if my math is right."

Kristen took a moment to process that information. It must have been hard to grow up without a stable home or a dad. She couldn't imagine, if she was honest, what it must have been like.

"That's really all there is. My grandmother passed away when I was ten, and no other family." He said it so casually but she noticed his jaw tense before he took another sip.

"Fair enough, your turn." She changed the subject.

"Why don't you tell people no?"

"I don't know. I just have always been a people pleaser. My mother was too, so I guess it was more of a learned trait."

"Shame Daniel didn't learn any of it."

They both laughed. Where Kristen couldn't tell anyone no, Daniel refused to say yes to anything. Until Macy, she'd only seen him attempt to please the woman he almost married, and even then, he didn't go too far.

"He got all the negative disposition for sure." She took her time with her next question, wanting not to bring the mood down again. "What's something you haven't done but still want to do?"

She expected an answer like visit Rome or something. Instead, she got a look. A look that melted her through to her core and sent a heat rising in her. His eyes held a seriousness to them but was somehow the most intense sexual look she'd ever seen.

Mike blinked once and reduced the glare, but she could see it was still there, behind the questions and the casualness of tonight. She knew, without a doubt, what he wanted, and she wanted it too, but wasn't ready to admit it to him just yet.

"I've never been one to hold back on my desires," he said, and she believed him. "Tell me, Kristen, you know that you can tell me no, right?"

"Wh—what do you mean?" She took a sip to buy time.

"I mean"—he stood and walked over to her, leaning down over her—"if you want me to leave, or stop, you can tell me. I won't be mad."

"I—" she began but Mike cut her off.

"You don't have to please me every time. If it's not what you want, tell me."

There weren't words, so she nodded to let him know she heard and waited for him to kiss her. He didn't, instead he took her hand, pulling her up from the chair and led her to the living room.

"Tonight, to answer your question, I'd like to lay here with you in my arms and watch a movie till we fall asleep. Is that okay?"

She'd never doubted for a moment that if she told Mike to leave, he would. He wouldn't pressure her, and somehow, she'd just always instinctively known that about him. The speech wasn't necessary, but it was appreciated.

"Honestly, Mike." His face fell as she began, "I'd love nothing more from tonight." Work could wait, she decided.

"Pick a movie. Do you have a bigger blanket somewhere?" He gestured to the small throw blanket on the couch.

"In the closet in my bedroom, on the top shelf."

He nodded and went in search as she glanced at the small couch and wondered how on earth they would both fit on there comfortably.

"Popcorn?" he asked when he came back with the blanket.

"Sounds good. I'm going to go change; you pick a movie." She practically ran out of the room.

The tension they were building was going to eventually come to a breaking point. She knew it, he knew it, and yet she was doing something she'd never done before: playing with fire.

It was dangerous and she'd likely end up burned, but Mike was doing a real number on her and she wasn't ready for it to end just yet. She changed into shorts and a T-shirt, leaving her bra on, something she wouldn't normally do to lay around, but she had company, she thought.

She debated washing her face, and in the end cleaned all her makeup off. Mike had seen her without makeup before and she didn't think it mattered to him. If it did, he was about to be disappointed, because she didn't wear it all the time.

When she returned to the living room, Mike was wearing sweatpants and no shirt. "Someone was confident about sleeping over," she commented as she popped a piece of popcorn into her mouth.

"Not confident, just prepared." He looked her up and down before commenting on her own clothing choice. "You sleep in your bra normally?"

Embarrassed at being called out, she shook her head and twisted the bottom of her shirt in her hand.

"If you aren't comfortable with me being here, don't do it, but you should take it off because I intend to be here with you all night." He didn't take his eyes off hers. "If not, come and get comfortable." He patted the couch.

Kristen warred with herself. On the one hand, she didn't want to sleep with it on. On the other hand, she didn't want to set any expectations for tonight.

"Hey, you decide. It's not a big deal either way. I just want you to be comfortable." When she still hadn't moved, he added, "I can help you if you want."

Just the thought of his touch sent a shiver up her spine. In the end she chose to return to her room and remove it. Mike was stretched out on the couch when she got back, propped up on one end. She needed larger furniture if he was to keep coming over.

"Come on." He dropped one leg off the couch and patted at his chest.

She sat down between his legs and laid herself back on his chest. He brought his leg back up onto the couch next to her. It took her more than a moment to relax, but when she finally did, he put the bowl of popcorn in her lap and grabbed a handful.

8

"My phone," Kristen reached for it vibrating on the coffee table.

"Too early," Mike groaned and rubbed his hand over his face to wipe some of the sleep away.

"It's just Macy. I'll call her back." He watched her look around and finally realize where she was.

Laying on top of him, they were both on the couch. Mike was half propped up by pillows and the arm of the couch and she was using his chest as a pillow, her back against him.

"You're probably uncomfortable. I'm so sorry." Kristen started to move.

"A little, but I like it here." He wiggled down as she did so he was a bit more stretched out. "You should get a TV in your room if we are going to continue this trend. I don't fit on the couch." He laughed.

"Or a bigger couch." Kristen teased and tried again to get up.

"Stay with me." He urged and helped her turn over to face him. "This I like a lot."

"Hmm. Not uncomfortable anymore?"

"Not at all."

Her face was directly above his now and it didn't take much effort on his part to lift his head and kiss her. Kristen followed him back down as he rested his head back and let her lead the kiss.

He could tell she was uncertain at first. Every move she made came with hesitation until her responded. He wanted her to be completely comfortable with him and resisted the urge to guide, instead letting her decide the next move.

The touched and tasted each other until he couldn't take it anymore, breaking the kiss to take a breath and calm himself back down some before he tried to take control from her. He turned his head to the side a took a steadying breath.

"You're going to be the death of me." He told her.

"Then we're even." She told him, smiling.

"I want to touch you." He told her.

She recognized it as the question it was and nodded. With a growl he had both hands on her, one pulling her mouth back to his. He reminded himself to be patient, to take it slow, but his hands weren't on the same page.

He slid his hands up her back and under her shirt, remembering as he felt only her skin that she was completely naked underneath. He shifted slightly under her, as his cock realized the same.

Slowly her lifted her shirt higher and higher, giving her a chance to change her mind. When there was no protest or hesitation he pulled it higher and Kristen backed away from him. He thought she was going to get up, but she studied him for a moment as he laid frozen waiting on her next move before removing her top and throwing it across the room.

"Kristen," he said before placing a hand on each one.

She moaned in pleasure as he kneaded her breasts under each palm. Collapsing on top of him, he kissed her again as she brought her mouth back to his. With his right hand he toyed with her nipple, feeling each reaction and committing it to memory.

"WHAT THE SHIT?" A voice startled them both.

Mike pressed the topless Kristen to him as he looked around to find Daniel and Macy in the doorway.

"Not now." He heard Macy say.

"What have we here?" Came another voice.

"Mom?" Mike asked aloud. It couldn't possibly be his mom, he thought. Please don't let it be.

"Beth called us here to talk wedding plans and we find you at this place with that, that—"

"Choose your next words very carefully." He threatened, his hands squeezing Kristen to him. "A little help here?" He asked Macy.

"On it." She started pushing people back as they came in.

Kristen's house was turning into a tourist attraction it seemed. The pillars could be heard from outside and he was also certain he heard Beth in the mix.

She scrambled off of him as the front door closed, retrieving her top from across the room. "Your mom?"

"I have no idea what's going on," he held up his hands in defense.

"I'm, umm.." Kristen gestured to her outfit, "not ready for company."

"Go get dressed. I don't know what's going on, but I think we will both want to be ready for it."

She went to her room and he picked up his bag from beside the couch to go get dressed as well. He found her in the hall when he was finished and took her hand as they walked outside.

One thing was certain, Daniel was going to kill him, or at least try, as soon as they were alone. He deserved it, but wasn't looking forward to it.

"Mike," His mother screeched, "What is going on?"

"I'd also like to know the same thing." Daniel added.

"Me too." Mike said.

"As I was saying," Macy tried to talk over the crowd, "it was very nice of Beth to invite you for the wedding, but we really didn't know you were coming."

The crowd, consisting of Daniel, Chris, all three Pillars, his mother, Beth, and Beth's mother all began talking at once.

"You know anything about a wedding?" Mike whispered to Kristen.

"I think it's ours, and Macy better thank her lucky stars she's pregnant because it's saving her life right now." She whispered back.

"Ours?" He asked.

"Come on Kristen, we have a dress to find today." Macy pulled at her other arm. "Sorry." She whispered to both of them.

"It's a women's day." One of the pillars shouted, and headed for the cars.

"I do love me a good wedding," another added as they walked away.

"Just go." Mike kissed her cheek and let go of her hand. She was safer away from his mother and Beth because he was about to get to the bottom of things and wasn't happy about it. "Text me?"

"I will." She returned his kiss and followed Macy to Daniel's truck.

The crowd he was left to deal with alone included Chris, Daniel, two mothers, and Beth.

"Someone explain, now." He yelled at the group.

"I'm taking Chris inside," Daniel told him and walked away.

"Son," his mother scolded, "what are you doing, about to marry Beth and now you're here with this woman?"

He glanced at Beth who was playing her part well, dabbing her eyes with a tissue and avoiding looking at him.

"I am not marrying Beth!" He yelled to the three women.

"What's the meaning of this?" Her mom snapped to him.

"I don't know. Ask your daughter. I didn't invite anyone here and I am not even seeing Beth. We have been over, for years." Running a hand over his hair, he let it drop to his side. "Well, Beth?"

"How could you?" She spouted.

"Could I what? Be honest?" He spat back. "I haven't seen you in years. I only recently saw you again, because I was with Kristen!" he was done with her nonsense.

"Mike, this is getting ridiculous." His mother came up on the porch.

"I couldn't agree with you more." He was still glaring at Beth, and reminding himself that he didn't want to go to jail because he was close to it right now.

"Whose house is this, and why are you here?"

He looked at her incredulously, had she not heard him? He was about to yell at them all when Daniel came out to join them.

"He's marrying my sister, didn't you hear?" He pointed at Beth. "I don't know who she is, but I assure you, he's not marrying her."

It was official, everyone had lost their minds. There was something in the water this morning that he and Kristen hadn't had yet because they were all crazy.

"Since when?" Beth yelled.

"None of your damn business." Daniel snapped at her. "Now, if you'll kindly get off my sister's lawn, we have preparations to do."

Daniel grabbed his shirt and pulled him into the house, locking the door behind them. They stood frozen there, staring at each other.

"Just do it, I deserve it." Mike told him.

"I can't do it if you're just gonna let me." Daniel grabbed his cane and walked away.

"Well, if you're not going to hit me yet, can you at least tell me what the hell is going on?" Mike followed, completely ignoring the three women still yelling out front.

"This might be better than punching you." Daniel said with a laugh. "Chris, go watch TV." He glared at Mike. "Sit on the floor."

"Nothing happened." Mike said.

"Right, because I definitely walked in on nothing."

"Fine, you want me to be the jerk?" He was beyond pissed at this point. "Nothing happened yet. Does that make you feel better?"

"Do you want me to punch you?"

"Maybe!" Hell a punch would be better than his mother being here.

"Come on, man." Daniel dragged his hand over his face. "We were at breakfast at The Diner this morning and, as usual, The Pillars invited themselves to talk to the new people that had come in. Well, they were looking for you, talking about a wedding."

"What the hell?" Mike dropped into a kitchen chair.

"So, naturally, they assumed it was you and Kristen because they'd already seen you spend the night here, or so they say?"

"They have." Mike admitted.

"I'm gonna kill you."

"You damn well might when you finish this story."

"So we raced over here to head them off because you know The Pillars take forever to get in their car. Now, it seems you and Kristen are getting married next weekend."

"No. Those things don't go together." His head hurt. None of this made sense.

"Yeah." Daniel put his hand on his forehead. "I'm supposed to take you out to do wedding stuff today now. I don't even know what that means."

"Chris!" Mike shouted. "Are those ladies still out there?"

"Yup!" He yelled back.

"Should we call the cops?" Daniel asked. "I mean, pretty sure I could take them all but I think Macy would get mad if I fought your mom."

"Not yet." He wondered if Daniel knew the whole story. "Do you know who Beth is?"

"Apparently your ex?"

"Kinda, yeah, but that's the chick that is a bitch to Kristen at work all the time. She's the reason she has the do the play and has been all stressed out."

Daniel blinked at him and processed that information before speaking. "Dude, only you."

"Yeah." He sighed.

"What are you doing with my sister?" Daniel finally asked.

"Marrying her apparently." Mike answered dryly.

"Before that."

Mike opened his mouth to speak before Daniel rushed to cut him off.

"Not exactly before that." He added.

He swallowed the laughter that was bubbling up before answering. "We are getting to know each other. I like her a lot, man." He stood to pace. "I can't say I didn't have long term thoughts when I started this with her, but this might have messed it all up."

Kristen wasn't going to just say no to everyone. He knew that about her and the last thing he wanted was to force her into anything. This was a mess.

"David's here! Can I open the door?" Chris yelled from the living room.

"I'll get it." Mike went to open the door for David. "Don't mind the crazy, come on in"

"Michael!" His mother yelled as he shut the door and locked it back.

"How long have they been there?" David asked.

"Too damn long." Mike led the way back to the kitchen.

David greeted Chris and then sent him back to the TV and joined them. "So, I hear we have another wedding?" His smile was lopsided as usual, always joking.

"Who knows?" Mike said.

"Nice to see you in one piece still." He told Mike before turning to Daniel. "Did you call me here to referee?"

"No, moral support."

"For which one of you?"

"Both." Daniel answered.

"Well, how do we get rid of crazy out front and who are they?"

9

———

Kristen was standing in the middle of a dress shop in what was quite possibly about to be her wedding dress, and had never been more confused in her life. Macy had given her the overview of what happened on their way here but she still hadn't processed anything.

She wanted to grab her phone and call Mike and ask him about it. Unsure how she felt about it herself, she hadn't tried yet.

Everything was in motion and she didn't know if she wanted to stop it. The last few times she'd been with Mike he'd been different, less flirty and more of a friend, but more than a friend at the same time. She was definitely falling for him.

If she stopped this, it would almost be like Beth won. It was terrible; was she about to get married just to prove a point to someone she didn't like anyway? That wasn't a reason to get married, she admitted to herself.

She could see herself married to Mike though. That was another thing making it hard to cut this act out right now. She had to admit that she loved the dress she was wearing and if she stopped trying to puzzle the whole thing out, she could see herself walking down the aisle to Mike. It was the most she'd ever daydreamed about a wedding since she was a kid.

"You look stunning," Macy told her.

"It's beautiful," she replied, and it was. The dress was strapless, fit her figure on top and then dropped down with a beautiful sparkling white princess bottom. It was big and she adored it.

"You should get it."

Kristen glared at her. "You know this is all fake, right?" she said through gritted teeth.

"Mine was too," Macy reminded her.

"It's not the same; we aren't the same."

"I didn't say you were."

"I'm ready to go home."

"Let me at least take a picture so you can think about it," Macy said, backing up.

She should have said no, but she wanted the memory of this could-have-been.

After she changed, she texted Mike to ask if the coast was clear.

Only just. David's here now though.

We are heading back now.

Are you okay?

I don't know. You?

Pretty much the same. I'm going to kick everyone out of your house and make us dinner so we can talk.

Sounds like a plan.

See you soon.

She put her phone away and looked out the window as Macy drove her back home. The Pillars had thankfully left midway through the dress shopping. They had grown bored and decided they had other plans.

"You know, I am sorry, it was just the first thing I thought of," Macy told her.

"I know, I'm not mad at you."

"You should be, I'm mad at me."

She didn't bother replying. The truth was that she wasn't mad, just confused now. She and Mike also had a lot of talking to do, and that was leaving her anxious.

The ride home felt shorter than the ride to the dress shop, and before she knew it, they were pulling up. David's truck was still outside, so any hope of having of avoiding everyone was dashed. At least the women had left.

Chris ran out to greet them as Macy parked the car. It would be weird next year when he wasn't her student anymore. She'd grown used to having him around at more than just Daniel's.

"I've been practicing my lines!" he happily told her.

"That's awesome! You're going to do great." She hugged him.

Inside the men were all gathered in her kitchen. The silence was deafening.

Daniel broke the silence. "We need to have a talk."

"Maybe, but not right now," Kristen answered. She had only one person to talk to and it wasn't him.

"It's coming though."

Kristen nodded and watched as Macy neatly managed him out of the room without anything else being said.

"I'd stick around, but this doesn't look fun," David told them and quickly left as well.

"So...," she said to fill the silence.

"Yeah." Mike brought one hand up to rub the back of his neck. "I pulled out some chicken you had in the freezer. Want anything special?"

Kristen shook her head. She wasn't even the least bit worried about dinner right now.

"Macy really went off the deep end, huh?" Mike asked.

"She apologized."

"Tell me what you're thinking," Mike prodded.

She stood and wandered the house, back to the living room, before taking a seat. "I don't know what to think."

"We don't have to do this just because she said it," Mike assured her.

"What do you want to do?" she asked.

She saw a quick smile cross his face before he let it drop. "I don't know what to do. I feel like I need to make one thing clear: I don't intend to ever get divorced, so if we do it, it's forever."

Kristen took the words and let them process before she spoke again. "I'm going to go shower."

Leaving him in the living room, she walked away, just needing distance to process her thoughts. She hadn't thought about divorce, but she could see where his feelings were coming from. Having seen his mother momentarily this morning, and after his opening up about her, she knew he was going to do all he could not to be like her.

She let the hot water run over her shoulders and melt away some of the tension she'd been carrying since this morning. It wasn't how she thought the day was going to go, that was for sure.

"Mike?" She had an idea and yelled for him as soon as she was dressed.

"Are you okay?" He busted in the room.

"I think I have a solution."

He put a hand to his chest and took a few breaths. "I thought something was wrong."

Kristen stood in the bathroom brushing her wet hair and watching him in the doorway. "I didn't mean to scare you."

"I know." She watched as he calmed down and some of the tightness in his muscles left his body. "What's your idea?"

"What if, we don't get married?"

"Oh." His whole face fell and that only helped solidify her idea.

"What if we fake it?"

"What do you mean?" he said hesitantly.

"Instead of having a wedding this weekend, we can sneak away and pretend we eloped. Then just come back and act like we were married."

"What about your name?" he asked.

"It's not like all women change their name, plus even if we did get married I wouldn't use it till summer so as not to confuse the kids with so little time left in the year."

It made sense, she thought. It gave them time to be with each other and see if this was even possible, in a way that wouldn't cause any judgement. It would get Beth to leave them both alone, and didn't make Macy a liar.

"It's solid, but I still feel like you're being trapped into this. I mean we've known each other for a while, but we just started this and I don't want you to feel pressured."

Kristen bit her lip. It sounded like he was against the marriage, real or fake. Somehow, she'd not thought that part through, and now she'd put her foot in her mouth with a solution that only benefitted her.

"We don't have to. It was just an idea." She picked up her lotion and started putting it on her face to give her hands something to do. "We can just tell everyone the truth. It's not a big deal." Focusing as hard as she could, she continued to rub the lotion in, not making eye contact with Mike.

"Kristen, stop." He knelt down next to her and pulled her hands away from her face. "I told you from the beginning I was looking for more. I don't want you trapped in it though. It should be our decision when we come to it."

"I don't really feel trapped. It's more that I don't want to tell Beth the truth but also that I can see this working." She felt herself blush.

"Then let's do it your way, but you have to promise me that you will tell me the truth if you want to end it, and not let Beth play a role in it?"

She nodded.

"I have one question though, how'd everyone get in this morning?"

Laughter bubbled up from her and she couldn't hold it back. "Daniel has a key."

"We're changing the locks."

"I doubt very seriously he will barge in here again. I think he learned his lesson there." She couldn't help it; it was funny. He was going to chew her out one day soon, but looking back on his face, it'd been funny now.

"Still, changing the locks." He leaned forward and placed a soft kiss on her lips.

"Okay. What are we going to do about your mom?"

"Nothing." Mike answered simply, like it was totally normal to just ignore your mother.

"We can't do nothing. She's here, so maybe we should have her for dinner?"

"It's not a good idea. She's.... rude."

"I mean she didn't seem friendly, for sure, but if we're about to be married maybe I should meet her on better terms." She felt her cheeks heat at the thought of how they'd been found this morning.

"If that's what you want, we will, but don't say I didn't warn you. Not today though," Mike said, walking closer.

"Definitely not today." She backed away out of instinct until she ran into the wall behind her.

"Where are you going?" Mike asked as he lowered his head to hers.

"I have no idea," she whispered.

"I've got one."

She expected him to kiss her. She expected to feel the warmth of his lips touch hers. She expected nowhere near what she got.

Mike brought his arms down around her butt and lifted her to meet his mouth. She gasped as he did and Mike took full advantage, sliding his tongue into her mouth immediately. She welcomed it and did her best to match his pace.

When he pulled away to breathe, Kristen whimpered and didn't recognize her own voice. She wanted to look around to see who else was in the room but never got the chance.

Pulling her away from the wall, Mike lowered her down to her bed and climbed over her. Panting, she couldn't seem to use her limbs, just laying there waiting for what would come next, fully anticipating him taking the lead. Surprising her again, Mike rolled over onto his back, changing their positions and putting her on top.

"Where were we?" he asked, tugging at the hem of her shirt.

Kristen collapsed on him as the doorbell rang. "Exactly here." She laughed.

"This is ridiculous," Mike said, sliding off the bed. "I'm going to punch someone in the face today."

Kristen laughed her way down the hall as Mike opened the door. It was like they were never going to be able to go any further. At least not today.

"What do you want?" Mike flung the door open.

"I saw your car here still and need to speak to you," his mother replied.

Kristen groaned and took a deep breath before joining him at the door. So much for not today, she thought.

"Hello, I'm Kristen," she greeted her.

"Yes, yes. Are you going to invite me in, or do you lack manners too?"

"I'm sorry, we haven't been introduced...." Kristen let it hang, waiting for his mother to introduce herself and putting the lack of manners back on her.

"Forgive me, I am Sharon, Michael's mother." She stuck out a hand.

Kristen took it and then used her hip to nudge Mike out of the doorway to let Sharon in.

"What a quaint home you have here." Sharon looked around at Kristen's clean but simply decorated home.

She wasn't embarrassed by it. It was small but she'd worked hard for it on her own and wasn't about to feel ashamed by that. She didn't have a lot of decorations, but that was her style. A few pictures hung in the living room but mostly her walls were bare aside from a mirror above the bench in the entry.

"I quite like it," she replied.

Kristen had a lot of experience with snotty women and knew how to charm her way out of being the bad guy in most situations. She couldn't say no in many cases, but could smile and charm.

"If you'll excuse us dear, I need to talk to Michael." She said flatly while not looking at her.

"She stays," Mike said before Kristen could reply.

"Well, then." His mother huffed.

"This"—she scoffed and gestured up and down at Kristen—"is fine for a first marriage but you need to be careful not to completely burn your bridges with Beth. You need to make things up to her."

"That's enough!" Mike stood and yelled at her. "Kristen is who I am marrying, not Beth, the end. I couldn't give a shit what Beth or her mother think of me. I never made, or intend to make, promises to her. If you don't like it, I suggest you leave."

She thought he would walk away, but he was in a battle of the wills with his mother, locked in a staring contest, which Kristen struggled not to find the humor in.

"I never," Sharon exclaimed.

"I know," Mike answered.

"We can be adults about this." Kristen jumped into the fray, trying to make peace. "Why don't we attempt to come to a common ground on things."

Sharon didn't like the teacher voice that Kristen was using and decided to stare at her with an eyebrow raised. Kristen wasn't having any of it though. She spent her days with cranky second graders that had summer-itis; she could handle one woman. Instead of staring back at her, which she knew was meant to make her cave to Sharon's will, she stood and walked over to her.

"I understand that you wanted something different for Mike, but I think that if you gave me a chance you might find that we can get along, might even like each other?"

Kristen kept her tone somewhere between hopeful and teacher to get her point across. There was no way that Sharon could get out of this now without being the one severely in the wrong, and while trying to intimidate her earlier was excused in some weird way because Mike made her stay, she was against a wall now.

"That was neatly done, dear," his mother informed her. It wasn't an acceptance, but she would gladly take it.

10

His mother had been politely rude the whole evening but had stuck around for dinner and Kristen had managed her quite well. She definitely could have been a society lady with the way she had neatly played his mother, putting everything she said back on her to make any response rude on her part.

She was always rude, but it was done in such a way that it wasn't openly visible. Backhanded compliments were her favorite thing. Kristen had taken them all with a smile and thanked her with a polite remark of her own.

He couldn't lie: he had been very impressed. After his mother had left, he had told her how well she had done. Kristen had simply laughed and let him know it had been pretty easy for her, if not comical at times.

They had spent the night together, neither of them attempting anything other than sleep. After the two failed attempts at something more, he'd not wanted to see what the third interruption would be.

Kristen was still in bed. He had made coffee but not started breakfast since it was so early, and was just sitting in the living room scrolling through his messages from yesterday.

He had a bid that he needed to complete by Monday evening and was reviewing that when Kristen joined him.

"I have so much work to do." She sighed and sat next to him.

"I know the feeling." Giving her a quick kiss, he stood. "I'll get you some coffee."

"I can get my own. You keep working."

In a flash she was up and out of the room. He just laughed and shook his head. It wasn't like it was hard to pour a cup of coffee.

"How do you like your eggs?" she yelled from the other room.

"Cooked," he answered.

It wasn't long before he smelled sausage and felt his stomach rumble. He tried to ignore it but quickly lost the battle and wandered into the kitchen.

"What are you doing?" he asked, seeing her standing at the stove stirring something.

"Making gravy," she answered

"You're joking?" That was his favorite thing, and he'd even been known to have sausage gravy for dinner a time or twelve.

"Nope."

She continued to stir and kept her back to him. He took advantage and slid up behind her, wrapping his hands around her waist and nuzzling her neck. Her heard her inhale sharply before relaxing into him.

"Go now; this takes attention." She swatted him with the towel.

"You can cook. I'll just be here." He nipped at her neck.

"I can't concentrate when you do that."

"That's what I like to hear."

He kissed her and backed away anyway. There was no way he was going to ruin his chances at homemade sausage gravy for breakfast.

A timer went off and Kristen looked around for a pot holder. He snatched the towel off the stove and reached in and pulled what appeared to be homemade biscuits out of the oven.

"Did you make these from scratch?" he asked, surprised.

"I didn't have any canned or frozen ones." She shrugged like this was normal.

He hoped it was normal; he could get used to this on the week-ends. She didn't need to win him over, but she had certainly cemented his resolve to make this work. It might be a fake marriage for now, but he intended to do his best.

When she had suggested they fake it yesterday, it had surprised him at first. She was turning him down, it seemed, but he decided it was a good thing. It wasn't a no. It kept her from being trapped and gave her an out for now. He just had to decide what they were going to do about living arrangements. It didn't make sense for him to keep his house, but he couldn't part with it if they weren't solid either.

Glancing up at her, Kristen was still stirring at the stove, but seemed to be almost done. This was something they needed to discuss right away. He also needed to get work done, same as her.

"Okay, it's self-serve because I don't know how much you want." She smiled and set a plate in front of him.

"All of it," he joked.

"I assumed as such, so maybe I should serve myself first?" She laughed and did just that.

He piled his own plate up and decided he was likely going to be in a food coma before he got any work done. It was probably the best breakfast he'd ever eaten. He tried everything separately and was surprised at how good the biscuits were on their own, though they were even better with the gravy and eggs.

They ate in silence, and he went back for seconds. Once he did, Kristen started cleaning up. He wanted to help her, but couldn't stop eating.

Once he cleared his plate, he did shove her away from the sink and help, even though he had to admit she'd done most of it. She laughed and left him to it.

He found her on the couch when he was done. "We need to discuss a few things," he told her, sitting down as well.

"That sounds ominous," she said, and flipped the TV off.

"Our living arrangements actually."

Kristen blushed. "I, um...."

"I was just thinking we would stay here, if that's okay with you? I need to get some things from my house, but I am not sure what to do with it in the meantime."

She chewed her lip. "Actually, I did think about this."

"You did?" She nodded. "And did you have a solution?"

"Maybe?"

"Don't leave me hanging."

"Well, David said the other night that he was thinking about moving closer to everyone. What if he stayed at your place for now?"

Mike thought it through. It was a solid idea. "That works." He grabbed her hand and pulled her on his lap. "Why didn't you ever tell me that you were this smart?"

"You never asked." She laughed and scooted back off him. "I want to say something that's probably going to make you mad, but I think it's important to start with clear intentions."

Mike held his breath at what she might say.

"I just, well, if we're going to be married, I—"

"What is it?"

"We should be only with each other."

"You mean no cheating?"

She nodded and bit her lip.

"You don't have to worry about that." He leaned over and squeezed her hand. "Is there anything else?"

"I need to make calls to stop the wedding plans," she told him.

"I should book us a flight while you're doing that."

"A flight?" Kristen swallowed and he kissed her neck.

"To Vegas. Where else would we elope to?"

"We don't have to really go."

He loved pushing her a little to see if she'd go for it. He didn't have any intentions of really doing it, just wanted to see how she'd react. Well, he would have done it if she'd gone for it.

"I'm kidding, we can stay at my house."

"Oh."

"You're cute when you're confused. Go call whoever, I've got some things to take care of."

He returned to his tablet while she went to the bedroom and did whatever she needed to cancel the wedding that was quickly being put together by everyone else. He responded to emails and was reviewing a design when she rejoined him, brow furrowed and chewing her lip again.

"What's wrong?"

"They planned a bachelorette party already and won't undo it."

Mike laughed. "When?"

"Friday."

"Well sounds like you will have a good time this weekend."

She threw the small pillow on the chair at him. "This isn't funny."

"Didn't you have one for Macy?"

Her eyes got big. "That's different."

"How?"

"It just is."

Mike tossed the pillow back at her and she caught it, sitting on the chair and holding it to her chest.

"Go have fun, you'll enjoy it."

She raised her eyebrow at him and he backed away with both hands up in surrender, still laughing. Her eyes darted around the room and he followed where her gaze landed, a glass of water that was considerably closer to her than him.

"You wouldn't."

Kristen raised an eyebrow. "You'll enjoy it." Her sarcasm heavy.

He didn't get to reply as she went for the glass and he tried to beat her there. He didn't and came up soaked for the effort. Kristen, on the other hand, was now curled on the floor laughing with the glass still in her hand.

"I will get you back," he told her.

"Worth it," she managed between laughter.

Laughing, he trapped her beneath him, knowing she was ticklish. "Was it?" he asked.

"Definitely." She laughed back at him.

Mike danced his fingers along her side, causing her to squirm and laugh harder. "You sure?" he asked again.

She didn't answer but continued to laugh and squirm as Mike switched hands and tickled her other side.

"Okay, okay. I give up, wasn't worth it," she said, still laughing.

"I didn't think it was." He kissed her forehead and sat next to her.

"I think I've had my workout this week now." She was out of breath as she sat up.

They sat there for a bit in silence on the living room floor, Mike's hair and shirt still dripping from the water. Kristen was the first one to get up and came back with a towel for him. He dried off best he could and then changed his shirt.

Kristen had all of her papers spread out on the living room floor again and Mike went back to his own work, but couldn't seem to focus. Instead, he watched her as she worked, tapping the pen on her lip when she was thinking hard about something and then scribbling something down.

Every now and then she would make faces at the papers in front of her. She would move from sitting to laying on her stomach and then sitting again as she moved papers from one pile to the next. It must be from working with younger kids, or maybe this was just her, spread out, comfortable, yet busy, and he liked it.

"What?" She caught him watching her.

"How do you work at school where you can't do all this?" He gestured to her stacks of paper.

"I don't, that's why it's here." She shrugged and gave him a look that said he definitely should have known that.

"Hmm" was his response.

"What are you working on?" Kristen asked as she got up and joined him on the couch.

"This building that we are starting on soon, I hope. Checking the plans and working up the full estimate."

He held the tablet so she could see and swiped around the building plans, showing her the parts that he liked, which made the building unique. She asked questions and followed along with what he was doing, zooming in on areas and then back out. He couldn't see her whole face, as she ended up curled next to him, but he imagined the faces she was making that went along with his plans.

"Do you want to go out for dinner tonight?" he asked as he noticed how late it was getting.

"There's going to be questions and staring," she cautioned.

"And PDA to make them talk?"

"If you insist." She laughed and spun in his arms to kiss him.

"We better not start this now on empty stomachs; you're going to need fuel in you for when we finally get there."

She blushed immediately but smiled.

11

———

*I*t didn't take them long to wrap everything up and head out to The Diner. She was nervous, there was no way around it. This was their first outing as a couple and she wasn't sure she was ready for the conversations that they were about to start.

Mike drove and she was becoming accustomed to climbing into his big truck. It was getting easier to do and with that she was slightly more graceful than she had been. He opened the door for her every single time which was something she didn't think she would get used to.

The drive to The Diner was shorter than usual, she mused as Mike parked. She waited for him to come around and open her door. He didn't like it when she did it on her own, while it was likely partly due to him being the gentleman, she also wondered if he was scared she might fall out trying to climb down.

As Mike shut the door, she took her first real look around. It was packed as was normal here for dinner, but especially so on a Sunday night. It was like everyone in town decided they weren't cooking on Sundays.

"Let's go get us a seat." Mike took her hand and she followed him inside.

It took them a minute, but they were able to grab a table near the wall as another couple left. She scooted in, thankful for the lack of people that had bothered them yet. Her thankfulness didn't last long, The Pillars beat the waitress over.

"Look at you two!" Ethel crooned.

"We were wondering how long it would take you to let her back out of the house." Mabel winked and Kristen cringed.

"Macy!" Matilda yelled. "Come take this lovely couples order."

Kristen didn't need a mirror to know how red her face was right now. She was positive it would rival a tomato and Mike was just sitting there cool as a cucumber chatting like they hadn't just announced their status to the whole town.

"Hey guys!" Macy strided over with her pen and pad in hand. "What can I get you?"

"I thought you weren't working anymore?" Kristen asked.

"Only when we're short staffed until the baby comes."

"Oh." She said quietly, she hadn't thought about her friend being here tonight, somehow it was more awkward than comforting. "I'll have the house salad."

"I will have the burger and fries."

"You got it. Two waters?"

Mike nodded and Macy left.

"Did our girl Kristen tell you about the party?" Ethel asked.

"A little, why don't you tell me more?" Mike prodded as she glared at him.

"Only a little though, you know it's a woman thing?" Matilda offered.

Mike nodded and motioned for her to continue.

"Well, you know we have to have a lot of sex stuff." Ethel confided.

"What?" Kristen yelled causing the whole restaurant to look her way.

"Hush now, you remember Macy's." Mabel shushed her.

The restaurant slowly resumed their conversations and all three ladies waited to continue their conversations until they did.

"We are looking for a stripper," Matilda told him. "If you weren't the fiancee I would definitely call you first."

It was Mike's turn to blush finally. "I don't know if y'all need a stripper."

"Nonsense boy, every good bachelorette party needs a stripper." Ethel swatted his shoulder.

"Besides, we couldn't get one for Macy, so she needs one too." Mabel told him.

"Needs one what?" Macy asked as she returned with their drinks.

Kristen tried to get her attention. Tried frantically to get her to retract the question.

"A stripper." Mabel said plainly.

"Oh, umm..." She looked to Kristen for help.

"You started this." Kristen sat back and crossed her arms.

"Anyway," Ethel moved on like this was the most normal conversation to have on a Sunday night in public. "There will also be lots of pink, drinks, and penis."

"No." Kristen and Macy said in unison.

"Hush. We are planning this and know what you need." Matilda informed them.

"Well, she can't get too drunk, we are leaving Saturday at lunchtime." Mike told them.

"She can take medicine." Mabel brushed off.

"This can't be real." Kristen moaned.

"Oh, ladies, I think your food is ready." Ushering all three women away, she got them back to their table and grabbed their food.

"We should have stayed in." Kristen told Mike when they were gone.

"Oh no. This was great, and we haven't even gotten our food yet." Mike teased.

"Any chance we can leave Friday?"

"Absolutely not."

She huffed and crossed her arms. She wasn't looking forward to Friday. Being the center of attention was not something she had ever yearned for and while it was fine when she was a teacher, it was an entirely different conversation for this situation.

"I mean, you're going to have a stripper, why would you want to miss that?"

First, she glared at him, and when that didn't get anything other than a smile from him, she looked away, only to see Beth approaching them.

"Well, if it isn't Mike and his whore."

"Beth, this is your only chance to walk away." Mike said through his teeth,

Gone was the man that had been laughing and teasing her. Instead the man seated across from her was hard, tense, and serious. She watched the muscles in his neck as he breathed and waited for her next move.

Beth must have seen the danger she was in because she opened her mouth to say something but spun around instead and walked away.

Kristen reached across the table and put her hand on Mike's arm. She felt the tension dissolve a little but he continued to watch Beth walk away and hold his stiff posture.

"It's okay." Kristen assured him.

"That was not okay, Kristen." He turned to face her and scooped her hand into his. "Don't ever think that is okay."

Surprised by the power behind his words, she nodded.

Mike released her hand as Macy showed up with their food. "Sorry guys, didn't see her walk in."

"You don't have anything to be sorry about. She's crazy." Mike told her and dipped a fry into his ketchup.

"She's a witch, that's for sure."

Macy left them to eat in relative peace. Every now and then someone would stop by and congratulate them. They both responded happily, but the true joy of the night was gone from Mike. She could see that he was still upset and decided to wait until they left to question it.

Mike set money on the table and rose, reaching for her hand

when they finished. More than enough for their meal and a really good tip for Macy. She smiled at the small gesture he would probably not admit to doing on purpose even if they were all friends.

They stopped to tell The Pillars good night but kept it short, breezing past Beth and her mother on their way out. Kristen had considered sticking her tongue out at them, but restrained. No need to provoke nonsense with such a childish gesture, but it was a near thing.

Once they were on the road, Kristen turned to face Mike. "What's wrong?"

"What do you mean?"

"She's a terrible person and that's not news, but why can't you move on? You were able to shut her down."

"She shouldn't have called you that."

"I can handle myself, it wasn't that big of a deal." She assured him.

"It was to me." He replied.

Kristen let it go, seeing that he wasn't going to and she didn't think that anything she said was going to change that. The rest of the trip was silent.

He helped her out of the truck but didn't follow her in. "You coming?"

"I need a moment."

Kristen unlocked the door and went inside, leaving Mike standing by his truck. Not knowing what else to do, she started getting ready for bed, hoping Mike would come inside soon.

She took her time but still climbed into bed with him still outside. She peeked out the window once to see what he was doing. He was just sitting on the tailgate of his truck, back to the house.

Nearly asleep she heard Mike shut the door and then head to the bathroom. Kristen laid still and waited to see what he would do next, only to hear the shower start. Rolling over to face the window instead, she relaxed, he was here and didn't look like he was leaving. She'd give him his space tonight then since he seemed to need it.

Surprising her, Mike slid into bed next to her and curled around her, holding her tight. She snuggled back against him and he held on tighter.

"Sorry, I just needed a moment."

"It's okay."

Mike kissed her hair and he'd her tight, she'd never been so secure and relaxed in any memory she had. "Thanks for coming back in."

"Always."

12

———

By Thursday, Mike was even more happy with his decision to be with Kristen. Waking up with her every morning was something he hadn't expected to enjoy as much as he did. They still hadn't managed to get to the next level physically, and while he was frustrated, he wasn't upset.

Every day this week they had gotten up together, taken turns getting ready, eaten breakfast and then went their separate ways for work. In the afternoons, Mike met Kristen at work and they would spend a few hours working on things for the school play.

Beth had been oddly pleasant to both of them since that night at the diner, and he wasn't sure why but it bothered him. He brought it up to Kristen who said it was weird but she wasn't going to poke at it and make it stop. She'd had a good point, so he let it go.

Tonight, they were sitting in the living room again working. She was spread out on the floor as usual and he was managing between his tablet and his phone to work on his latest project and keep a sharp eye on their bottom line.

"Have we decided where we are going tomorrow?" Kristen asked.

"Nice try, but it will be Saturday."

"Ugh." She threw a piece of popcorn at him.

"You'll have fun. You did at Macy's."

"That's because I was not the center of attention."

"It's only fair."

"Shut up." Sitting up, she started gathering the papers she had been grading. "Really, though, where are we going?"

"I was thinking just back to my place since I need to pack some things up anyway and it's far enough away to be gone."

"Oh, that'll be fun. I've not really been to your place."

Mike sent her a questioning look.

"I mean I haven't since we, you know." Blushing, she went back to her papers.

"No, tell me. What do I know?"

"Shut up." She laughed.

He set his tablet and phone down on the table before pulling her to a stand. Once she was on her feet, Mike bent down and hooked his arm behind her legs, scooping her into his arms.

"Put me down!" she yelled with laughter.

"Nope, all mine," he said as he carried her down the hall to their room.

It had stopped being her room last Sunday when he'd crawled into bed with her and she'd snuggled close. There was no chance he'd ever be able to sleep again without her tucked neatly against him.

He laid her gently down on the bed and slid over her until their faces met. Kristen relaxed under him.

"I missed you today," he told her as he planted kisses on her neck.

"We weren't apart for long," she reminded him.

"Too long."

Before she could say anything else, he took her mouth in a kiss that she quickly answered. He felt like a teenager laying here with this beautiful woman kissing on the bed and nothing more.

"Mike," she said as they broke apart for air. "I want you."

Those words were all the encouragement he needed. He raised back and pulled off his shirt, tossing it to the floor. Kristen raised up and did the same, followed by her bra.

He stared in awe of her. Her breasts were there on display for him, and they were everything right now. "Perfection," he said as he cupped one in his hand and set his mouth to outlining the other in feather-light kisses.

She moaned and arched towards him as he teased her. He let his breath pass over her nipple, avoiding what they both wanted for a little longer to see how far he could take them both before giving in.

"Mike, please."

That was all it took, as far as he could take it, no more waiting. He took her nipple into his mouth and Kristen cried out in pleasure.

"God, yes," she whimpered.

He soon replaced his mouth with his other hand and made sure to give the other breast the same leisurely attention as they both fought to take steady breaths. Taking a chance, he teased her nipple with his teeth, looking up to gauge her reaction.

Her mouth fell open and her head tipped back as she pushed her breast closer to him. He smiled to himself and continued to tease them both.

"Mike... I can't...."

"You can."

"I need you."

"We're just getting started," he promised as he kissed his way down her body and just under the waist of her pants.

Kristen writhed beneath him and moaned as he did. He never imagined her as a noisy lover, but he loved it. Every moan, whimper, and cry was encouragement for him. His cock strained against his jeans, begging to find the noise as she moved beneath him.

He slid one hand over her pants to her heat, cupping her as she continued to move. Adding pressure, Kristen rode his hand as she begged him for more.

When she'd had enough, she pushed his hand away and began unbuttoning her pants. "Now," she demanded.

He agreed. They'd been building to this for so long, he didn't think he'd be able to push himself any further either. Standing, he dropped his pants and boxers to the floor.

Kristen said something he didn't quite hear as she watched him undress. "What was that?" he asked as he joined her in bed again.

"I want to touch you now," she told him as she slid her hands down his abs.

He grabbed her hands and pinned them above her head. "If you touch me right now, I promise I won't last for a second."

She giggled and pulled at her hands.

"Not a chance."

Slowly he angled himself over her, finding her slick entrance with the tip of his cock. She stopped pulling at her hands as they both held their breath, waiting for this moment to finally happen.

He thrust into her in one motion as she yelled his name. She was so wet and warm that he could hardly keep a thought straight in his head. He wanted to make this as good for her as it was for him, so he held still, taking a deep breath and letting it out to restrain himself.

Kristen, on the other hand, didn't want to wait. He'd only just recovered his senses when she started to move beneath him.

He let go of her hands, but was happy to see she left them where he had pinned them, and grabbed her breasts, pinching each nipple gently and then harder as he pulled out and slid back in again. Kristen cried out again, even louder this time.

"Oh. My. God. Mike," she said each time.

He wasn't going to last long, he knew that, so, taking charge to get her where she needed to be, he released her breasts and shifted her hips to put her legs around him. He reached up and grabbed her right hand, pulling it down to feel her wetness.

"Touch yourself," he demanded, immediately regretting it as she looked at him with uncertainty.

She blinked as she watched his face and began to do just that as he started to thrust once more.

"Do it, Kristen. Come for me," Mike urged as he alternated between watching her face and her hand.

"I can't."

"You can."

He was getting rougher now as he neared his own peak. Seeing

Kristen approaching hers, he took one nipple into his mouth, squeezing it with his teeth, and she came apart. He felt her quiver as he finally let himself go, collapsing on top of her as her contractions pumped every bit from him.

Panting, he rolled over, taking her with him.

"I've never," she started. "Holy cow." She gave up on words.

He laughed and she swatted his shoulder.

"I'd hit you harder, but I don't seem to have muscles at the moment."

"Let me get us cleaned up." He rolled her off of him and rose. "I'll be right back."

Finding a washcloth, he ran it under warm water as he cleaned himself with another one. Wringing out the one for her, he returned to the bed to help her get cleaned up before putting it back in the sink.

She'd blushed prettily as he did, and he was happy to learn her blushes went all the way down her chest and didn't think he'd ever recover from that image. Screw every guy that had ever touched her and never did the little things for her, because the fact that he'd turned her head as he'd helped her get cleaned up said this was a new experience for her.

"Mike?" she asked as he pulled the covers down to get in the bed.

"Hmm?"

"I may never recover."

"Me either, but neither of us have to tonight."

She curled up around him, her head on his chest as he stroked her back and played with her unkempt hair.

"Tomorrow's a big day though, so you better get some rest." He couldn't help but tease.

"Shut up, Mike," she told him on a yawn.

13

*D*espite the fact that she had no desire to go to a party tonight, Kristen woke happy. She and Mike hadn't moved throughout the night, and she was still curled up next to him when she opened her eyes.

Turning the alarm off, she stretched and felt the soreness of her muscles. Ones that hadn't been used in longer than she'd like to admit.

"Morning," Mike said as he stretched and rubbed a hand down his face.

"Morning," she answered. "I'm going to go shower if you want to sleep a bit longer. I'll wake you when I get out."

"I'll start the coffee." He tossed the covers back and searched the room for his boxers.

Kristen couldn't help but laugh as she watched from the safety of the blankets.

"You could help." He rolled his eyes and tossed her shirt at her.

"I'm good here."

She wasn't moving either. It was one thing to be caught up in the moment and completely naked, quite another to walk around in the morning.

"Don't get shy on me now," Mike teased as though he could read her thoughts.

"Go make the coffee!" She made a shooing motion with her hand as he slipped on boxers.

"I'm going. So demanding."

Kristen laughed again, and as he left the room, she couldn't help but think it was weird waking up with laughter. Normally she was a morning person, but having someone to laugh with or tease her was different, and she was starting to really fall for this man.

With that thought, she did get out of the bed and take a shower. Mike had coffee on the dresser for her when she returned to the bedroom, and moaned as she took her first sip. Today, she needed it.

"Did I hear my name?" Mike joined her in front of the mirrored dresser.

"You know you didn't."

"Hmm, seem to remember that being my name last night."

"Stop it." She tried for firm but it came out on a laugh.

"I'm going to shower now." He kissed her forehead and left her to get ready.

Kristen quickly put her makeup on and dried her hair some before tossing it up in a ponytail. Mike never took long and was back in the room before she was done.

"Tonight's the night."

"Don't remind me."

"Penises, pink stuff, the Pillars, what's not to love?"

"All of that together, that's what."

"I'll leave it alone then, for now." He paused and pulled a shirt over his head. "I'll see you after work and then when you get home, okay?"

She nodded and they both went to the kitchen. Mike tossed her a yogurt that she barely caught, not ready for it.

"Mike!"

"Just testing your reflexes." He shrugged.

"I'm gonna test your reflexes in a minute."

"Oh yeah? What are you going to do?"

Mike cornered her. She desperately looked for a way out, but he'd called her bluff. He slowly lifted her shirt just enough for his fingers to dance across her ribs, causing her to jump and laugh.

"No. Don't." She laughed as he continued to tickle her. She did the only thing she could think of and smeared her yogurt across his face.

Complete shock crossed his features as his jaw fell. He's stopped tickling her but she was still laughing, for a different reason now.

"Did you—" he broke off and backed away just enough for Kristen to slip away and take off down the hall.

"This isn't over." He laughed as he followed her, wiping yogurt from his face with his hand.

"It's a face mask!" She laughed from the bedroom. "People pay money for those." Her stomach hurt from the laughter and she was curled on the bed as Mike laid next to her.

"Truce?" he offered.

"Deal."

After that, Kristen still had the giggles. They carried her out the door and throughout her day at school. Somewhere between the anxiety over tonight and the students, a bubble of laughter would creep up and spill over as the image of Mike completely shocked with yogurt on his face entered her mind.

The week had actually gone so well she'd forgotten about Beth and her nonsense for much of the day. It wasn't to last though. As she packed up her bag for the weekend, Beth showed up in Kristen's classroom.

"Heard a rumor about you," Beth said as she entered and sat one hip on the table.

"Couldn't care less." Kristen continued to pack.

"I heard you aren't getting married for real."

She froze, just long enough to get a laugh out of Beth. "Believe what you want."

"Oh, I will. I also know that if you don't marry him then he's still fair game."

"A relationship, married or not, is not fair game." Dropping the last stack of papers onto her desk, she looked at Beth. "Why would you want someone that isn't interested in you anyway?"

"Posterity, of course." Picking up a pen, she started twirling it between her fingers. "He's the only reason I'm in this town. We were supposed to be a power couple, and he's come to slum it with people that aren't even close to our tax bracket."

She wasn't shocked. She wanted to be, but she wasn't. It was interesting the way some people thought, and she wasn't going to be the one to try to change her mind.

"I'm leaving now. Get out." It was probably the most rude she'd been to her.

"Whatever. Just know that before it's all said and done, he will be with me and not you."

Kristen shrugged. "Mike is a grown man. You do realize that, right?"

"Oh, I know, probably better than you do."

Kristen was following Beth out her classroom only to have the door shut on her. She had some choice words but decided it wasn't worth it tonight. She was doing something that Beth wasn't, going home to Mike, and that would be enough.

Macy called on her way home to remind her she was driving tonight. As of now she had no idea where they were going, very little information on who was going to be there, and was absolutely terrified at the idea of the party.

At Macy's bachelorette party, it had been loud, at The Diner where people could see them and half the town had come, though it was likely every female over 18 had been invited.

By the time she pulled up at home, she'd conjured a million different scenarios in her head, each one worse than the last. Mike was on the porch waiting for her with a big smile.

"You ready for tonight?" he asked.

"Stop asking questions that you already know the answer to."

Mike laughed. "It will be okay. You'll probably even have a good time."

"Shut up. I need to go get ready and pack for tomorrow."

Kristen brushed past him and into the house, heading straight for the bedroom. Mike was on her heels and as she reached up to get her rarely used suitcase down from the top of the closet, he was there, taking it from her.

"I can get it."

"I know, but I can help." He set it on the bed and turned to face her. "Are you really that upset about tonight?"

"Honestly? I'm just nervous." She sat on the bed, calming down a little. "I had a run-in with Beth as I left too, and that hasn't helped things."

She watched Mike tense and could see the anger practically radiate off of him.

"What did she have to say?"

"Somehow she knows we aren't really going to get married this weekend."

"How would she know that?"

Kristen shrugged. She had no idea. "I didn't confirm it, but it did catch me off guard. She said some other stuff about if you aren't married, you're still fair game and crap."

"What is that even supposed to mean?"

"That she doesn't know you at all?"

"I haven't told anyone we aren't really getting married," he confided.

"Me either. Even Macy doesn't know."

"I'll—"

"You'll do nothing," she cut him off. "If you do, she will know it's not real and at this point I just don't want to deal with her on it."

"It's still weird she would guess that."

"I know."

Kristen's phone started ringing and she pulled it out of her pocket and showed it to Mike before answering.

"Hey."

"I'm on my way."

"I'm not ready yet."

"Better get ready then." Macy laughed and hung up.

"Ugh." Kristen went to the closet and pulled out a dress. "I'm going to get ready. I guess I'll pack in the morning."

She didn't take long to change and was putting a fresh face of makeup on as Macy arrived.

"Mike let me in," Macy said as she walked in.

"It's fine. I'm almost ready."

She watched in the mirror as Macy moved around her room before sitting on the bed. "It's so weird to think you're getting married tomorrow and you won't let any of us be there."

"I told you I don't want anything big." Macy tried to steady her hand while she put eyeliner on.

"Oh, I'm not fussing or anything. It's just crazy you and Mike will be getting married and that the next time I see you, you'll be married."

"I hadn't thought about that."

"But tonight we celebrate your last free day!"

"Pretty sure I'm already in a relationship."

"You know what I mean."

"Ladies," Mike greeted. "Macy, may I have a moment with my fiancée before you steal her away?"

"Sure." Macy shut the door behind her.

"What's up?" Kristen asked, finally ready to head out.

Mike took her in from head to toe. "I'm rethinking this being a good idea."

"Shut up." She swatted his arm and reached in the closet for shoes.

"Not kidding."

She turned to look at him. His eyes were glued to her and she knew what he had on his mind. Instead of being proper or assuring, she lifted her dress to present him with the black lacy thong she had on under her short, fitted black dress.

"Macy might have to wait a while longer," Mike whispered as his hands slid down her body.

"Nope, you insisted I go, so you get to wait."

Mike nipped her ear and then kissed the spot, sending shivers down her neck and arms. She wanted nothing more than to stay here with him, but a commitment was a commitment and she'd have to head out with Macy to her bachelorette party.

"I'll wait up," he whispered before letting her go.

"I—I don't know how late I'll be," she stammered, trying to recover her voice, which apparently fled with the goose bumps.

"I'll wait anyway."

"Kristen!" Macy yelled.

"That's my queue." She backed away from Mike and nearly fell into the closet.

"Go on then."

Kristen nodded and left him there in the room. Macy was waiting by the front door for her to leave.

"Come on, we're going to be really late."

Kristen rolled her eyes, grabbed her small clutch and stuffed her phone inside, not bothering to lock the door behind her as they left.

"**W**here are we going?"

"My old place," Macy answered.

"You're joking."

"Nope. It was a good place to have it and more private than the diner."

"Well, I guess, but like at least there was a lot of seats and stuff."

"It's going to be fine, trust me."

The last thing she had at this moment was trust in her friend. She knew this night was going to be extra and there was nothing she would be able to do to stop it. Instead, she resolved to go with the flow and attempt to enjoy herself.

"Macy," she said as she took in the number of cars lining the driveway, yard, and road.

"Calm down."

"I am calm." She wasn't, but saying it helped, a little.

Matilda was at the door before she could open it. "Come in, you're late!"

Kristen's arm was taken as she was pulled into the small house with entirely too many people packed in.

"Let's get you something to eat," Mabel said, taking her other arm, "and drink."

She looked back and forth between the two women, who were oddly missing their third. Both were dressed in floral prints as usual, this time in pink flowers. While each woman normally stuck to some version of their own colors, she struggled to reconcile their new matching look.

"Do you like our dresses?" Matilda asked.

"Umm, yes?" Neither woman reacted to the doubt in her voice.

"Here, make yourself a plate. We have tons of food here; don't want you getting too drunk before the entertainment arrives." Mabel shoved a paper plate in her hand and started piling food on.

"Entertainment?"

Rather than answer, Mabel simply winked at her. "Eat up. Matilda, get her a drink."

"No, wait, what entertainment?"

Completely ignored, she was swiftly put in a chair with a plate in her left hand and a pink-colored drink in her right as both women disappeared. Panicking a little, she set her drink on the floor and picked at her food as she looked around for a clue that there wasn't going to be a stripper.

She didn't taste it but had somehow managed to finish her plate by the time she managed to get out of her thoughts. All three Pillars were headed towards her with a lot of pink things in their hands.

"These are for you!" Ethel was also in a pink dress, but it was definitely slightly shorter than it should have been for a woman who was pushing eighty and was usually in her Sunday best everyday.

She slipped a sash over Kristen's head and lifted her arm to straighten it out. Glancing down, she read "Bride to Be" on it. A tiara was held up in front of her; it was pink, sparkled, and had two penises on it with a wedding ring in the center. She didn't have time to take it in before it was placed on her head.

"Did you see the ice?" Ethel asked.

Kristen shook her head and picked up her drink to see little ice penises floating inside of it. She tried to take a breath and choked on it.

"Were you sucking on the ice?" Matilda asked, patting her back.

Caught somewhere between laughter and humiliation, she couldn't quite stop the coughing. Matilda continued to thump her back as Kristen struggled to get herself together.

Finally able to get a full breath in, she looked around the house from her vantage point. There were pink decorations everywhere screaming "Bride to Be." If they didn't say that, there was a penis on it.

"Screw it," she said mostly to herself and tipped her drink back. One rogue piece of ice floated forward and bumped her tooth. "Hard dick," she said, sending the Pillars into a fit of laughter.

"That's our girl." One of them applauded.

"I don't think you even noticed what you ate, if the ice shocked you." Mabel shook her head.

"Not really."

"You had wrapped weiners, penis-shaped pasta salad, meatballs, three different eggplant dishes"—Mabel leaned over and nudged her with an elbow—"that's what they call penises in today's language."

"Show me," she said, and stood up. At this point she was intrigued and really wished she had looked harder at her plate before eating it. Knowing her luck, she probably toyed with a penis shaped piece of pasta on her plate while everyone watched.

She looked over the food offerings and laughed herself silly. The only thing she hadn't eaten yet was the charcuterie board that had toothpicks holding the meat rolls onto two balls of cheese.

"Have you seen the dessert table yet?" Macy said as she joined her.

"There's a dessert table?" Kristen shook her head and continued to laugh.

"Come on."

Macy dragged her out back where someone had set up an impressive spread of penis-themed dessert, including a cake with a smiling pink penis drawn on it waving at her and holding a flag that said "come and get it."

"That one has a smile and arms." She pointed out the cake to Macy.

"That's the least creative thing here."

There were chocolate-covered bananas with a sign that said "safe is better." Two bowls in the shape of penises held small chocolate and fruit candies. There were penis-shaped cookies that had been decorate to include veins and hair on some of them. At the end there were a bunch of suckers in the shape of penises with another sign that said "for practice."

Kristen picked up a cookie and bit into it.

"You aren't supposed to use your teeth." Macy fake scolded her.

Kristen let out a breath as she choked on air and spit cookie all over the floor. "Oh my God."

"What? You should at least lick the frosting off."

"Girl!"

"Look at the plates and the table cloth."

"Is that penis-shaped confetti?" She picked one up to look at it and noticed the tablecloth was also covered in cartoon penises. "Where the hell did you guys get this?"

"Wasn't me for most of it. I did find the plates though."

"Are those plates in the shape of—" She didn't even bother to finish as she picked one up. "Where?"

"Online."

"What the hell is wrong with you?"

Macy laughed. "This is tame, at least you don't have a giant inflatable one."

She was right. There had been that one floating around at Macy's party and she'd just be grateful not to have anything that big.

"What's the entertainment that the Pillars mentioned?" Kristen remembered to ask, a little scared.

"I don't know."

"Macy!"

"I really don't."

"Did they actually get a stripper?"

"I hope not."

"Me too."

Kristen tipped her drink back and finished it off. "I think I need another."

"I'm jealous."

"I have to make it through this somehow."

Kristen refilled her drink and sent a text to Mike telling him about the penis-shaped pasta and sending a photo before putting her phone away again. She and Macy walked around, greeting all the women they knew, and Kristen accepted a lot of congratulations.

Women she'd known her whole life were there, some sucking on penis-shaped suckers, and Kristen didn't think she'd ever recover from the sights.

"It's time!" Ethel yelled out the back door and pulled Kristen into the living room and onto a chair in the middle of the room.

All the women stood around the outside of the room, looking at Kristen. She was looking around for some hint of what was going to happen when the music started. It was a slow, sexy song that she knew. As the beat picked up, she watched as women parted and a man dressed as a cop appeared from the front door.

A whooshing sound went through her ears as she struggled to keep her seat despite being thoroughly embarrassed. She crossed her legs and tried to look as unapproachable as possible in a sash and a penis crown.

"I hear someone's getting married!" he yelled over the music and cheering women, as everyone pointed at her.

"That should be a crime, shouldn't it, boys?"

Two more men dressed as cops joined him as Kristen prayed for invisibility.

"Sounds illegal to me. We should search her before we arrest her."

The music changed to something much more upbeat and way more raunchy as the men started dancing around her and making sure to include the crowd too. It was a blur of hip movements and some pretty impressive dance moves, where they slowly lowered themselves to the floor and back up again.

The song changed again and this time she had all three men dancing on her. At any given moment there was at least one real penis entirely too close to her face. They stripped as they danced, encouraging her to touch them, although she awkwardly declined, keeping her hands to herself.

This went on for at least two full songs until they started to work the crowd more. Women she only knew from church were putting dollar bills in these men's shiny G-strings. It was a confusing mix of laughter and horror.

It was when all three men each took a Pillar to entertain that she completely lost it. Someone gave her another drink as she left the chair in the middle of the room and made her way back to Macy.

"Are you seeing this?"

"It's like a train wreck; I want to look away but can't," Macy answered without looking at her.

That was probably the best way to describe it, Kristen agreed. She tipped her drink back while keeping her eyes fixed on Ethel, who was waving a twenty dollar bill in the middle of the room, sitting in the chair that Macy had vacated.

Ethel was rewarded with a dance that will haunt Kristen's nightmares for the rest of her life. The little woman in her too-short dress with pink flowers on it was rubbing her hands up and down the abs of a stripper before taking a peek in the G-string and leaving her twenty dollars in there and then letting the band snap back into place.

"Nope," Kristen said to Macy, who was standing beside her, mouth open wide in shock.

"What did I just see?"

"How do you clean your eyeballs?"

Kristen looked around at the other women who were cheering loudly; none seemed as surprised as her. It was like she was in the twilight zone and she wanted out.

Thankfully the next song involved a sexy cleanup of their clothes from the floor and a police hat was placed on Ethel, Matilda, and

Mabel, as the men danced their way out of the room. The room slowly began to clear out some.

"We are cutting the cake in a few minutes!" Mabel yelled.

"Did you enjoy yourself?" Ethel asked. "I did." She raised her eyebrows a few times making sure her innuendo was noticed.

"Oh. My. God" was Kristen's response, and she tipped back her drink.

"What? My honey hole might not get any action but that doesn't mean I can't appreciate a good male specimen."

Drink spew from her mouth and she did her best to aim for the floor but still managed to get some on Ethel. "Sorry."

"It's okay. I didn't realize you were so shy."

"Something like that," she sputtered.

"Let's go cut the cake!" Matilda led the way to the cake table.

Thankfully that was the wildest part of the night and nothing else too crazy happened. After the cake was cut and handed out, people started to leave. All in all, the party had only been a few hours and she was glad it was clearing out and nearly over.

"Did you see the confetti?" Mabel asked as they started to clean up.

"I did. I'm impressed at the number of penises at this party." She was, it had definitely gotten an A+ for creativity.

Mabel tossed a handful over Kristen's head. "You have been blessed with good sex for your marriage."

At this point very little would shock her. "Can confirm," she answered.

"That's our girl!" Mabel laughed.

"I think I need to go home." Kristen giggled, thinking that she'd never be able to accurately explain this night to anyone.

15

———————

Mike was waiting for Kristen on the porch when Macy brought her home. She was laughing but didn't seem to be too terribly drunk, able to walk at least. He assumed she'd get trashed since she didn't want to be there.

"I have seen things that cannot be unseen" was her greeting to him as she walked past him into the house.

She slipped her shoes off the second she walked in, dropped them by the door, and went straight to the bedroom. He followed behind her, mostly curious at her statement and to see what she was up to next.

If he expected to be entertained, or that she might come home and want to finish what he started earlier, he was about to be very disappointed, as he watched her pull the dress over her head, toss it across the room, and climb into bed.

"You good?" he asked.

"Am now. You can't imagine the horror I witnessed tonight."

Confused, but since she was clearly okay, Mike retreated and left her to sleep. Instead, he went back to the living room where he had spent most of the night until he knew she was on her way back. He sat there for a while and picked his phone up a few times intending to ask Daniel and Macy what happened, but always setting it back down instead.

After a bit, he joined Kristen in bed and held her close, deciding he could wait till tomorrow to find out what happened.

He woke to Kristen tapping on his arm.

"Let go," she said frantically.

He did and she sprung out the bed and out of the room. He stretched and tried to wake the rest of the way up, unsure of what was happening. He was still laying there confused when she came back, wearing nothing but that pair of black lacy thongs, and quickly dove under the covers.

"Everything okay?"

"I had to go," she answered.

"Oh." He got her meaning and started to laugh.

"I wouldn't have woken you up but I was a little trapped."

"You're fine. It's probably past time to get up anyway."

"No. It's early." She settled back into the bed and cuddled up against him.

"The sun coming through the blinds says otherwise."

"Fine," she said, and rolled onto her back to stare at the ceiling.

"Wanna talk about it?"

"Believe me when I say that you most definitely do not want to hear about it."

"Were there strippers?" He knew that it really didn't matter, and even if there had been he didn't need to be worried when it came to Kristen's loyalty, but he couldn't stop himself from asking. He had a jealous streak that he didn't like admitting to.

"Three." Kristen rubbed both hands down her face. "Things happened that I wish I could unsee."

"Three strippers?" he asked, shocked.

"Yep. One for each Pillar."

Mike rolled over to face her. "You're joking?"

"No. This is too crazy to make up."

"What—No, I think you're right. I don't want to know about that part."

"Smart man."

"Tell me more about the penis pasta."

Kristen laughed and rolled herself out the bed. "You make the coffee first. I'm going to go shower."

He waited for the shower to start and then got himself out of bed and slipped on a pair of shorts before heading the kitchen. Once the coffee was started, he checked his phone and flipped through a few messages before landing on one from his mother letting him know she'd be staying at his house for the next few days as she was having a disagreement with Beth's mother. They'd known each other for as long as he could remember, but they often got into small squabbles with each other. He quickly called her back.

"Hello, Michael."

"You can't just stay at my house without asking," he told her.

"You aren't even going to be in town; what's the big deal?"

He let out a breath, not bothering to pull the phone away from his face. "You still can't just invite yourself to use my house. What if someone else was staying there?"

"Like who?" She sounded intrigued, like she was on to something.

"David is going to be staying there and should be back in town at any time."

"Well, if he shows up, he can stay in the other room until my flight."

"That's not the point, you don't just invite yourself to use someone else's house."

"I'm your mother, you should want to help me in my time of need."

"This isn't a time of need. You could get another hotel room."

"You would rather me stay in another strange place by myself than in your home?"

"That's not what I said."

"Then tell me what you mean."

"It's fine. Whatever. Use the house. Don't leave a mess."

Mike ended the call and jerked his arm back to toss the phone before finally relaxing instead. He'd have to find another place for them to go now, and at the last freaking minute.

He was looking up flights to Vegas when Kristen came in search of her coffee.

"What's wrong?" she asked as she made her coffee.

"We have a big problem." He quickly explained the conversation with his mother.

"How do they know we weren't really getting married?" Kristen asked when he was done.

"What do you mean?"

"This is awfully convenient for her to want to stay at your house, and Beth to say what she did. It's like they know."

"There's no way for them to really know that though."

"I don't get it either." She hugged him and sat down on his lap at the table. "Where are you thinking we go instead?"

He didn't answer and just showed her his phone.

"Vegas? You're joking."

"No. You already have Monday off anyway; we could go have a good time," he pressed.

"That's expensive." She bit her bottom lip.

"Not too terribly. Besides, I'm paying, so don't worry about that part. Just say yes."

"Why not? Let's go." She stood and sipped her coffee, leaning against the counter.

"Earliest flight is in a few hours. How quickly can you be ready?"

"Won't take long, maybe half an hour to pack."

"Go start packing. I'll book the flights."

Kristen squealed when he smacked her butt as she walked away.

He focused the next half an hour on getting everything booked. He had them a flight, hotel, and limo from the airport in no time. He didn't flaunt it, but he'd been raised wealthy and knew about traveling very well. He hadn't done it in a while, which really only meant he had no miles to redeem. But a weekend in Vegas with Kristen? it'd be worth it no matter the cost.

She was still packing when he finished so he tried helping her. However, it only took a few attempts before he was shooed from the room for getting on her nerves.

The majority of the rest of the day was a blur. They'd made it to the airport with little time to spare, immediately boarded, and the look on her face had been worth everything when she realized they were flying first class. He hated flying business class and didn't go lower than that. It was several hours of your life; you should be at least somewhat comfortable.

He was happy for the light meal, as he realized neither one of them had eaten since yesterday. Kristen chatted about the plane, the view, even the chairs as they flew. He hadn't seen her that excited, and it made him happy to watch the joy on her face.

The flight was almost seven hours, and after the second meal, they both dozed off for a bit, waking up when the plane was close to landing. Kristen was in the window seat taking in the sights and urging him to look as they neared Vegas.

He'd pointed out a few landmarks when he saw them and waited for the plane to land. He probably should have picked somewhere closer so he could just have her all to himself. It looked like this weekend was going to playing tourist instead of in bed where he wanted to be. If everything worked out with this fake marriage though, he'd have a lifetime to spend in bed with her instead.

Her face when she saw the limo was priceless. She was practically glowing.

"Are you joking?" she asked as the driver put their bags in the car.

"Not at all." He held his arm out for her to get in first.

"This is insane." She climbed in and slid over to make room for him to sit beside her.

"Just sit back and look out the window, unless you want to start the party early?" He pressed a button, revealing a bottle of champagne on ice.

"Stop it." Kristen smiled wider than he'd ever seen. "Is this real life right now?"

"Of course!"

Mike pulled his phone out of his pocket and snapped a few photos of her before she took it from him. Spinning it around, she snapped a few of the both of them and then sent them to herself.

"This is unreal."

He had no regrets about this trip and definitely should have considered it from the start. Her enthusiasm was contagious as she pointed out things she recognized and sometimes included the movie she had seen it in.

"Mike." Her tone was cautious. "This is too much."

They were pulling up in front of one of the most well-known, luxurious hotels in Vegas. The driver opened the door and he slid out, reaching back to help Kristen out.

"Let's get checked in." Silently he hoped they didn't mention the total, which was not a big deal to him, but he knew she'd probably be upset if she really knew what the total was.

"Mike." She leaned over to him as they waited to check in.

"Kristen, just enjoy yourself, the cost is not your concern."

"It's that much?"

He'd meant to ease her mind but apparently that only made it worse. "I promise, this is not a big deal. Enjoy it."

She bit her lip again as she did when she was worried or overthinking things. He put his thumb there and gently eased her lip out of her mouth before planting a kiss on that lip.

"This is for us," he whispered.

Check-in was smooth and they were in the elevator headed to their room.

"I know the timing is off here because of the time zones, but I'm hungry," she confessed.

"Me too, actually. This whole day has been a bit of a rush." The elevator dinged and they stepped out on their floor. "Do you want to go see the sites and eat out, or stay in?"

"I don't know."

She looked a little overwhelmed as they walked down the hall to their room, so he let it go. She might be a little more surprised once she saw the room he booked.

He'd spared no expense on their trip this morning. If they were going to do it even for a short trip, they were going to do it right.

The suite opened up to dark hardwood floors, clean lines, and white furniture in a sitting room right off from a white kitchen. Everything shined to a high polish and the view showed off all that Vegas had to offer with floor-to-ceiling windows.

"Mike...." Kristen slowly walked around, touching things in awe as she did.

He walked in and grabbed the tablet sitting on the counter and dimmed the lights, flipping on the gas fireplace. It wasn't magic, but from the look on her face, it definitely was something like it.

"Okay. This is the best hotel room I've ever seen." She smiled at him. "Where's the bedroom?"

Mike walked over to the black door and opened it wide for her to look inside. The bedroom had another fireplace, the same set of windows, and a massive bed in the middle of the room anchored by two nightstands with lamps.

Kristen dropped he bag and laid down on the bed. "This is the most comfortable bed I have ever laid on."

Mike laughed and set his own suitcase in one of the two chairs by the windows. He opened the last door in the room to the massive bathroom which contained a tub that could easily fit four people. One long counter with two square sinks lined the wall on one side, and a shower that rivaled the tub in size stood in the back corner.

"Are those rain ones?"

He looked around until he caught what she was talking about: the two showerheads. The massive glass doors meant no privacy, but he was thinking of a different situation.

"Wanna try them out?" He raised his eyebrows to make sure she didn't miss his inuendo.

"Um, yes!"

She didn't even hesitate and started tossing her clothes on the floor as he turned the water on to warm up for them. She was laughing as he nearly fell trying to get out of his pants.

"You won't be laughing in a minute," he teased.

"Bet!" She laughed.

Mike picked her up, squeezing her butt as he did and carried her into the shower.

16

———

They had made love in every room of the massive suite for the remainder of the night, and Kristen was sore all over in the best possible way. She had showered alone this morning and worked to get the tangles out of her hair from not brushing it after their shower last night.

Mike was laying on the bed, watching her move around and pretending to scroll on his phone.

"I know you aren't playing on your phone." She slid into bed next to him.

"Maybe not," he conceded, and set his phone down. "What do you want to see today?"

"Hmm, I like you, but maybe something besides this amazing hotel room?"

"Okay, fine." He faked a sigh and got up to take his own shower.

Kristen wandered around, taking in the room and the view, and opening every cubby and cabinet she could find. The room was fully stocked with anything you could think of for entertainment; there was even food in the fridge. She helped herself to a yogurt while she waited and continued her self-guided tour.

There was even a bookshelf on the wall next to the massive TV, which was really more of a home theater than a TV by sheer size. She looked through the books there and noticed something for almost anyone. It was unlikely anyone was laying around in this room reading a book, but it was a nice touch.

"Tell me I haven't bored you into a book instead?"

"I would not need to be bored to read a book."

"No, likely not." Mike came up behind her and dropped his arms around her. "Ready to go explore?"

"Almost, are we walking a lot?"

"Maybe, why?"

"Shoes." She'd brought sensible and she'd brought cute, but those were not the same.

She slipped away from him and pulled out her sensible black flats to go with her white shorts and black top. The sandals with their tall heels looked back at her as the clear choice to set her outfit off, but she ignored them, shutting the suitcase. The last thing she wanted on this trip was blisters.

They made their way through the hotel and out into the heat and sun on the strip. Mike led the way, and by dinner she was stuffed, tired, and felt like she had done every tourist thing possible in Vegas except gamble, and the one thing that had been on her mind since Mike had mentioned Vegas yesterday, visiting a chapel.

She'd thought about it every time they'd passed one, and in Vegas, that was a lot. It was nothing she'd talked to Mike about yet, but the more they were there, the harder she thought about it. She wanted to marry Mike. This fake marriage was something she was growing more comfortable with everyday, but was he still feeling that way? Was it enough?

They'd known each other for years now. It wasn't like this whirlwind romance was really starting out as two people that didn't know each other. They'd just really gotten to know each other better over the last few weeks, and the more she learned, the more she realized each part had her falling in love with this handsome man that flirted too much but still made her feel like the only woman in the room.

"What's on your mind?" the man on my mind asked.

"Just thinking."

They were sitting near a fountain with ice cream cones that she had insisted on, but they were far bigger than she expected. There was no portion control here; everything was huge.

"What are you thinking about?" Mike used his thumb to smooth her forehead where she knew she showed her worry.

"You," she confessed, looking at her ice cream.

"That's a pretty serious face for thoughts about me." His tone was light, but she could feel his gaze on her and it was more intense than his tone.

"Just thoughts." She took a bite of her ice cream while she debated what level of honesty she wanted to go for here.

"Kristen." His tone urged her to look at him.

"I just... I don't know."

"If something is bothering you, I'd rather know so I can help, especially if it's about me."

Kristen looked around at the people moving past, but the two of them were alone, no one noticing the couple sitting there. It wasn't a private setting, but it was just them at the same time.

"I want to make this real," she whispered.

"I don't think I heard you, Kristen. You're going to have to say that again." Mike dropped his ice cream in the trash next to them and crouched down in front of her.

Kristen took a deep breath and held his gaze. "I've been falling in love with you, Mike. I want to get married for real."

Mike didn't say anything and just looked at her.

"If you want, that is. If you don't, it's no pressure at all." She started to backpedal her thoughts. Maybe it had been too soon.

He took her ice cream and tossed it in the trash with his, before returning back to her again. "How long have you been thinking about this?"

Well, in for a penny.... "Most of this week." No point in lying to him. It had been on her mind constantly since she woke up yesterday.

"You're serious?" He took her hand in his.

"I was, but if you want to wait, I don't mind." She tried to pull her hand back.

"Let's go back to the room."

They didn't speak on the walk back to the hotel. Her kept her hand in his, but that was the only thing that made contact. Kristen chewed her lip and stopped and then started again.

She tried a few times to take her hand back, her palms getting sweaty with each step they took. As much as she wanted to question him about what they were doing, she couldn't bring herself to ask the questions for fear of rejection.

He'd wanted this, or so he'd said before all of this started. Maybe now that they'd gone this far, he'd changed his mind. Did he not see himself with her for the long haul now that they were together for real?

Maybe the stunning women that they'd passed who had sent longing looks at him had changed his mind. If he wanted to be free instead, she'd rather he told her in private anyway, so she walked beside him back to the room.

"Wait right here," Mike said as they walked into their sitting room.

She was too confused and worried to do anything other than what he'd asked, so shewaited. Mike went into the bedroom and came back out in probably less than a minute, but it felt like forever as she stood there not knowing what to do or think.

Always one to overthink a situation, this one was no different. When Mike returned, she closed her eyes and braced herself for his rejection, but it didn't come. Slowly she opened her eyes to find Mike standing directly in front of her.

"Kristen, I've wanted this longer than you know."

Mike bent down to one knee in front of her. He opened a small black box that had been in his hand and pulled a ring from it as Kristen tried to keep herself calm.

"Marry me, right here, right now?"

She didn't have any words; her voice was completely gone, so she nodded. Nodding caused the tears that she'd been holding back to drip freely from her eyes and down her face.

"Yes?" he asked.

"Yes, Mike. I will marry you right now," she managed.

He grabbed her left hand and slid the ring on. She waited for him to stand and then threw herself at him, wrapping him in a hug and pressing her lips to his.

When she pulled back to wipe the tears from her face, Mike looked down at her.

"I love you. I want this too."

Every bit of her that had been trying to stop the tears gave up, and they flowed in earnest now. "I love you too, Mike. Let's do this."

"Let's do it."

Mike grabbed his phone and made a few calls to find a chapel that was available as she attempted to redo her makeup to not look like she'd been crying, which was no easy feat. When she was done, she changed into one of the dresses she'd brought with her.

She'd only brought two and one had been white. It was more of a beach dress, but it would work and it looked good on her. It was unfitted, off the shoulder, and flowed as she walked. This time though, she went with the cute shoes.

"I found a place if we can be there in the next hour," Mike spoke as he joined her in the bedroom. "Well, someone got ready faster than me." He walked to her and held her hand up for her to spin in her outfit. "You look wonderful."

"You can't kiss me, or say anything nice right now. I'll cry again, and we don't have time for me to get cleaned up." She shooed him off her with a giggle.

"Nothing nice?"

She shook her head. "Not until after."

Mike laughed at her and pulled out his suitcase. "I'll be just a minute."

He slipped into the bathroom, and Kristen took the time to adjust her hair in the mirror. She put it up and then let it back down again, trying a few different styles before optioning to leave it down and set it with hairspray instead.

She looked as Mike left the bathroom in a black suit that fit him perfectly. Not expecting the perfection that he'd pulled off with a change of clothes and likely just a comb in his hair, she felt her jaw drop. He looked good in anything he wore, but seeing him in a suit and walking towards her, she struggled to believe this man that could have any woman had chosen her.

The black pants had small stripes that moved perfectly with his body, showing his lean lines as he walked. His jacket was a work of art, the way it subtly showed off his muscles despite hiding them all beneath its lines. His white shirt was accented by a simple black tie, but it all worked perfectly together.

"You'll catch flies." Mike touched one finger to her chin and pushed her mouth closed.

He pulled her to a stand and then spun her to look in the mirror with him.

"We're going to turn heads tonight, my dear," he whispered, looking into her eyes.

"You certainly will," she added. She wasn't trying to put herself down in any way, but this man was perfect tonight.

"You ready?" he asked.

"Let's go get married." She took his offered hand as they left the room.

It didn't take long for them to get to the chapel, which made sense as there were a million of them to choose from in Vegas. Nerves were starting to get the best of her as they filled out their paperwork in the small office off the chapel entrance.

"You just put all your information on here and then sign the last page," the woman told them, pointing out where to do each.

"Of course," Kristen nodded, not looking up. She'd gotten nervous enough now to have completely blanked on her own personal information.

"Are you okay? We can change our minds," Mike whispered.

"I'm fine," she said automatically.

Mike set his pen down and looked at her. "I really only want to do this if you want to with me."

"I do! I just—" She could feel the blush creep up her face. "I forgot my address," she mumbled, reaching into her clutch and pulling out her license.

Mike pressed his lips together in an attempt to hide his smile, but the edges of his mouth turned up despite his efforts. He took the form she was putting her information on from her and filled in her address.

"Thanks." She tipped her head back down to complete the form, keeping her eyes off him.

When they were finished, the lady took the forms and typed some things in the computer as the couple sat there awkwardly, trying not to fidget. Kristen took the time to study her as she typed.

The woman was older, jovial, and dressed to the nines for a wedding ceremony. Definitely her Sunday best, complete with a small pillbox hat to match the light-pink dress she was wearing. To keep her mind off her nerves, she wondered what it would be like to do this every day.

"Okay, you're all in the system. The only thing left to do now is the marriage bit, and we can get your certificate signed." She stood, prompting Kristen and Mike to stand as well. "You go in there, and my husband will meet you at the altar." She gestured to Mike.

Before leaving, he kissed her sweetly on the lips and gave her hand a reassuring squeeze.

"Now, my dear"—she faced Kristen—"do you need to freshen up or anything?"

Kristen thought about it and shook her head. It hadn't been that long since they'd gotten ready, so there was nothing to touch up.

"Okay, good. Once we hear the music, I will walk in with you or you can walk in by yourself, whichever you prefer."

Kristen clasped her hands together in front of her. She wasn't prepared to make any decisions once she got here. The woman must have seen the indecision on her face.

"It's okay. I can walk with you." She patted Kristen's tightly clasped hands. "You two are going to make it. I can tell and I am never wrong."

Kristen felt a small smile find its way out. "Thank you."

"Of course." Just then the wedding march song began and the lady held one elbow out for Kristen to take. "That's your cue, dear."

The doors opened for them, and Kristen took a steadying breath as she looked around the chapel, taking in all the flowers and the empty pews until her gaze finally landed on Mike at the end of the aisle. Mike held her gaze, never looking away as she walked down that aisle as though there was no one and nothing else in this world except for the two of them.

His smile grew the closer she got. Her nerves were gone as the lady handed her arm to Mike, and she took the step up to stand behind him and face the man performing the ceremony.

The vows were short and sweet, from what she remembered. It was like an out-of-body experience, and she couldn't quite come back down from it, as happy as she was, floating on cloud nine. They signed another paper and then took several photos and announced their wedding to Macy and Daniel before heading back to the hotel, both of them grinning ear to ear.

17

He could hardly believe it. Yesterday, he and Kristen had gotten married, and it was because she had wanted to. He'd brought a ring, but only because if they were to fake getting married, she needed to return with one. She was on his mind when he bought it, and he'd taken the time to pick one out that was just for her.

She'd stared at it on their ride to the chapel. It had taken a little convincing, but she'd finally snapped a few photos and sent them off to Macy. There was an immediate and excited response.

When calling to find a chapel, he was as picky as he could be on short notice, opting for something other than Elvis. Something with a little more class for them.

They'd gotten the highest package, which included a bouquet for Kristen and a single flower for his jacket, with a name that he couldn't remember. There had been lots of photos that they had posed for, and many more had been taken as they said their vows.

He was flipping through them now on his phone as Kristen slept curled into his side with her head on his chest and her leg wrapped around his. He laughed a little when he got to the photo they'd taken with Macy and Daniel on video call. They had all been smiling and laughing, and it had come out great, definitely a keeper.

"I like that one," Kristen mumbled.

"I thought you were asleep."

"I was, but I wanted to see the pics too." She finished on a yawn.

"Go back to sleep."

"Nope."

Kristen wiggled her body up his and pressed a kiss to his lips.

"I love you."

"I love you too."

She smiled up at him, and he wondered if life could get any better than this moment right here.

"Well, wife, what should we do before we catch our flight?"

"Hmm, see, I should want to spend my last day here exploring the town, but I think there are other things that I want to explore right now."

"Oh, really?" He slid his hands up her leg, stopping on her hip.

His phone rang, pausing what they were starting. "It's my mom," he said, and answered the phone.

It was just as well; she was getting hungry, so she slid out of the bed and walked to the kitchen to find some food. She started the coffee and was debating how hungry she was as Mike walked out of the bedroom.

"Everything okay?" she asked.

"She's lost her mind, but other than that, yeah."

It was clear morning sex was going to be off the table now. Whatever she had said had upset him, so she switched gears. "Want to go get breakfast instead?"

"That sounds great, after coffee."

She didn't press for more information on the call, assuming he would tell her when he was ready. She poured them both a cup of coffee and then headed for the shower to get ready for the day.

When he didn't come join her, she had to admit she was a little disappointed. She knew something was up from the call with his mother, but she didn't expect him to not be able to push it from his mind. Holding her head up and smile in place, she decided it wasn't going to ruin their day.

"Your turn," she told him as she left the bathroom.

"I won't be long." He gave her a peck on the forehead as he walked past, but seemed distracted.

Kristen busied herself getting ready and left him to do what he needed. Grabbing her phone, she texted Macy while she waited.

Good morning!

How's it feel being married? Shouldn't you be otherwise busy this morning?

His mother called and ruined the mood.

I can see how that would happen. Are you still coming home today?

Yep!

Dinner tomorrow? I think Daniel will be back in town early.

It's a date for sure.

Mike stepped out ready to go for the day, and they left for breakfast. He had no place in mind, and they stopped at the front desk for advice. Finally settling on one place, they caught a cab to what was supposedly the best breakfast place in town.

He'd been quiet on the ride there and, other than ordering, didn't have much to say.

"What's wrong?" she asked, ignoring her earlier resolve to not bother him about the call.

"It's just my mother. She knows how to press some buttons, and I let her this time."

"Want to talk about it?" Kristen pressed.

Mike heaved a sigh and looked up from his phone. "She wants to know how long this marriage is going to last so she can start planning the real one."

"Is that it?" This wasn't new; she'd been like this all week.

"She took Beth to meet my father."

That one got her. She'd been putting syrup on her french toast but stopped mid pour at that news. "Your father?" She didn't know anything about his father, only that his mom remarried often.

"Yeah." He leaned back in the booth and slid one hand down his face.

Kristen swallowed back all her feelings on the situation, from not knowing about his father to being jealous, which was irrational, reminding herself that it was about his feelings right now. "Do you have a relationship with your father?"

"A strained one at best. I get along with my mother better."

"Oh."

"Yeah."

"So, what happened in this meeting?"

"Apparently she introduced her as my fiancée, and now I have messages from him congratulating me on sowing my oats first because she seems like a handful." His phone dinged again and he held it up to show her the messages.

I told you I am not marrying her. I'm already married.

Everyone thinks their first marriage is the one that will last, but it's not.

I'm not doing this with either of you. I am not interested in Beth regardless of my relationship status.

Don't burn that bridge. She can open a lot of doors for you.

Fuck off.

Don't start like that with me. Just know your options.

"Ouch," Kristen said when she finished reading them. It was starting to really hurt her feelings now. "Can I see your phone?"

Mike raised an eyebrow at her but handed it over. She went into the contacts and turned the notifications off for both his parents before handing it back.

"You can just ignore them now."

Mike's face turned up in a smile for the first time since the phone call this morning. "Did you just block my parents?"

"No, just muted them."

His laughter started as a giggle until it was loud enough to turn heads. "Just like that, huh?"

Kristen shrugged. "I mean, why not?"

"Why not indeed." He was still smiling as he paid the bill and held his hand out for Kristen as she slid out of the booth.

"I can undo it if you want," she said quietly.

"No, this is great. It's just that you can sometimes forget that you don't have to answer and be available to everyone all the time."

"Sometimes I lose it on purpose so people can't ask me to do things," she admitted.

"I would never have guessed."

They waited for the cab and headed back to the hotel. Mike was much chattier this time and pointed out different landmarks as they drove. She looked and listened but was also distracted by the messages and conversations today. It was hard to admit that they really didn't want their son to marry her.

"We can pack and then have lunch before we have to leave if you want."

"I'm not really hungry, since we just ate," she reminded him.

"Oh, sorry."

"You didn't really eat, so if you want to stop somewhere and eat, I don't mind." He had mostly just pushed things around on his plate for their breakfast instead of eating anything, distracted by his parents' drama.

"I was a little distracted." Mike grinned sheepishly. "Why don't we go for souvenirs instead? And I will grab something at the airport before our flight to eat."

"Are you sure? I don't mind stopping for food." She didn't want him to skip a meal simply because she ate when he didn't.

"I'm fine," he assured her.

"If you're sure? I wouldn't mind picking some things out for everyone."

They gathered their stuff and headed down to the lobby. There was a small gift shop next to the reception and Kristen took her time looking through everything. She settled on a few gifts and paid for them while Mike walked around, looking at things but not picking anything up.

"You ready?" he asked as she took her bag from the clerk.

"I think so."

"Our ride should be here any time, so we can head out and wait."

"Did you get another—"

"I did. Only fair we leave the way we arrived."

Kristen shook her head as they walked. Sure enough, a limo was there waiting to take them to the airport. She had to admit it was nicer than a cab, but it wasn't necessary either. Shoving the practical side of her brain away, she concentrated on enjoying the experience instead.

She took in all the sites she could on the way to the airport. Mike spoke little but mostly remained his stoic self. Hoping he would shake it off, she left him to his thoughts and did her best to ignore her own.

18

———

*I*rritated didn't being to describe how he felt the next morning. His parents had both messaged and called all night. He was grateful Kristen had muted their alerts, but he still saw the missed notifications when he opened this phone.

They were both insistent on this not being a lasting marriage. This only guaranteed that, whatever happened between them at this point, he wasn't even going to leave her. Not that he planned to ever do that, but it drove that point even further home.

He was laying in bed as Kristen showered, getting ready to go back to work. He felt like an ass because he couldn't quite shake the mood his parents had put him in. It's not even like his father was an active person at any point in his life, or that he cared what he thought.

It had been a long flight home last night, and he knew he'd been too quiet for all of it. They'd been too tired from the flight to do anything when they got home except pass out.

Getting up, he started the coffee for them and had a cup ready for her when she was ready.

"Good morning, wife," he greeted as she walked in the kitchen.

"Good morning, husband," she returned. "Is that coffee? You're a saint."

He felt the smile spread across his face; she didn't seem to be angry with him. "Hardly, but I appreciate it anyway."

"Go get ready." She shooed, grabbing an apple off the counter and taking a bite.

"Yes, ma'am," he joked, and did as he was told.

She was just finishing it when he came back out of the bedroom. They had agreed he would take her to work today so he could finish working on the set this afternoon and they would only need to take one car home. Well, not even home, they were headed to Daniel and Macy's for dinner, and Kristen seemed excited by it.

"Ready?" he asked.

"Not really." She groaned, but took her bag and headed out to his truck.

She talked about the play on the way to the school to fill the silence, he assumed. Tonight, he'd show up with flowers to make up for his mood, he decided as they pulled up to the school.

"Can I walk you to your door?" he asked.

She sucked in a breath, clearly caught off guard by his request. "Umm, sure."

He took her bag from her as she climbed down from his truck. "I really need to get something lower to the ground, huh?"

She blushed a pretty shade of red. "I think I can manage."

"I do like to watch you climb up in it."

Her blush deepened, and he bent down for a deep but short kiss, mindful of where they were. When he backed away, it took her a moment to steady herself, and he couldn't help the grin on his face, loving that he had that effect on her.

"Stop it," she scolded with a playful swat on his chest.

"Maybe we should call out today."

"I'm already here at this point. Come on." She spun on her heel and walked to the school, Mike catching up quickly with his long legs.

He set her bag down behind her desk where he'd seen it before, and she immediately began pulling things out and spreading them across her desk.

"How was the wedding?" Beth's voice interrupted his thoughts. The way she'd said wedding had him turning to look at her.

"Our wedding was great," Kristen answered.

"I'm sure it was. Any reason why you had to run away to get it done?" Beth prodded.

"To keep you away," Kristen mumbled, not loud enough for Beth to hear.

"Can we help you?" Mike asked her.

"I was just wondering when Kristen would be changing her last name?"

"When she—" Kristen cut him off.

"As soon as school is over for the summer and I have time to get it done. Anything else?" Kristen was using her teacher voice, something he loved hearing from her as she asserted herself, which she didn't do near as often as she should.

"I know this is fake." Beth sneered.

Mike had one hip on Kristen's desk, turning his head from woman to woman, watching everything unfold. They seemed to have forgotten he was there.

"You don't know anything," Kristen threw back, and finally stood, putting her hands on her desk and leaning forward. "Get out of my classroom before I report you."

Beth's mouth opened and closed a few times, reminding him of a goldfish. She turned and walked out as he struggled to keep a straight face.

The moment she was out of view, he let out the laughter he'd been holding.

"It's not funny," Kristen told him, but he could see the smile turning up the corners of her mouth.

"It really was," he assured her before kissing that mouth. "I love you. I'll be back this afternoon."

"I love you, too."

He left her there, smiling back at him. Quickly walking through the building, he prayed that he didn't run into Beth. Managing that feat, he quickly climbed in his truck and headed to work.

He texted Kristen throughout the day and was happy to know that Beth had left her alone. Something needed to be done about her and the rest of the people he knew all bashing on Kristen.

After inspecting the job site and finding everyone where they were supposed to be, he drove to his house. Well, not just his anymore.

"Oh, you scared me," his mother said as he walked in.

"This is my house still. Not sure why you are surprised to see me."

"I thought you'd be staying with your—"

He could feel the next word: it was in her tone and it wasn't going to be a nice one. "Wife?" he asked.

She rolled her eyes but didn't argue.

"I came to let you know that you need to find another place to stay today. Tonight, this house will be occupied." David was coming back early, and he was happy to have a reason to get his mother out of his house.

"I'm so glad you changed your mind, let me call Beth and let her know." She moved to pick her phone up off the table.

Mike put his hand over it. "I am not coming back here. Daniel is renting the house from me. And you need to get out."

"I can't just leave. I have plans." She dismissed him.

"You can, and you will. I didn't tell you that you could stay here, and had you asked you would have known."

"He can just stay in the other room. It'll be fine."

"You aren't listening to me. David is renting this house, you need to leave, and he's not looking for a roommate."

"Don't be silly. He won't mind." She swatted her hand in the air as though it was that simple.

"I will remove you. I don't want to, but I will." He crossed his arms and waited for her to make a decision.

"You aren't serious."

"I am. Very."

"I never." She brought her hand to her strand of pearls that always graced her neck.

"You have made enough problems since you got here to last a lifetime. I can't make you go home, but I strongly suggest it." He opened the front door. "I expect you out of here by four."

With that, he shut the door and ran a hand through his hair. He was done with her shit and hoped she really did head home and take Beth's mother with her, but knew it was unlikely.

He drove straight from there to the school to catch up with Kristen before school let out completely. Hopefully if he was there, he could keep Beth away from her for today at least. It wasn't a permanent solution, but he was going to do what he could.

He parked and watched as kids were shuffled into busses and cars and left. Kristen found him in the parking lot, joining him as she put the last of her kids on the bus.

"Hey handsome." She hugged him.

"I missed you today."

"I missed you too."

"Ready to do this?"

"Nope, but I'm going to anyway."

Mike grabbed his tool bag out of the truck bed and took Kristen's hand in his other, walking side by side into the school.

As they were almost to the stage, Kristen stopped him. "I wanted to tell you that I did something today and make sure you were okay with it."

"I did something today too." He leaned against the wall.

"I took off a day next week to go change my name on everything," she said quietly.

"Are you sure?" he asked, getting excited.

"If you're okay with it?"

"Okay with it? Nothing could have made me happier." He picked her up and spun her around.

"Put me down!" She sounded stern but the smile on her face told on her. "What did you do?"

"Nothing as amazing as that." She arched a brow at him. "I kicked my mother out of my place."

"Oh. Umm… I thought we would stay at mine, but that's okay, we can pack tonight the things I'll need." She stumbled.

"For David, remember?"

"Oh."

"Yeah, oh. I'm not changing anything about our living arrangements. This is closer to your work, and mine moves constantly so it works fine for me."

"I forgot." She tucked her head. "It's been a long day."

"I agree with that sentiment. Let's get this rehearsal underway, and I will get back to my props and we can get to dinner." He took her hand, pulling her with him to the stage where the kids were waiting.

"Oh, one more thing: I told Macy we would take Chris home."

"Okay."

It didn't matter to him if they took Chris home. That's where they were headed anyway, so it didn't make sense not to do it. Besides, he loved Chris, even though he could talk more than anyone else.

Kristen smiled at him and then started gathering the students into their places. Mike was left painting mostly by himself, a kid would wander over now and then, but the next two hours passed pretty quickly. Once this coat of paint dried tonight, he would have only one thing left to do and he'd be done.

Kristen wasn't so lucky, and he figured he'd likely be here anyway trying to come up with something to keep himself occupied as she prepared for the play.

Once the last kid was with their parents, he picked up Chris and carried him out to the truck with Kristen behind him. Once he had Chris buckled in, he helped Kristen up, giving her butt a squeeze as he did. She nearly fell as she turned to give him a shocked look.

"Couldn't help it." Mike shrugged, making no apologies.

19

———

"I still can't believe it." Macy hugged her as she walked in. "Go do your homework," she told Chris.

"Fine." The quiet kid was really coming into his own since they'd moved here. Unfortunately, that meant his attitude was also getting intense.

"Don't give her any sass," Daniel scolded.

"I wasn't," Chris threw out as he ran to his room. He wasn't going to stick around for anything else.

"I swear he used to be nicer."

"They tend to do that as they grow up," Kristen assured him.

"Come on, let's head out back." Macy ushered everyone out.

"There they are!" David jumped up and thumped Mike on the back before hugging Kristen. "You sure you made a good decision?" he asked loudly enough for everyone to hear.

"It was the best decision." Kristen came around the table to where Mike had sat, meaning to sit in the chair next to him but finding herself pulled onto his lap.

Everyone laughed as he did. She felt herself turning red and struggled to get up.

"If you keep doing that, neither of us are going to be able to get up," Mike whispered.

She froze, instantly catching his meaning.

His chuckle had her ducking her head to hide her embarrassment.

"Man, let my sister go," Daniel defended her.

"Never," Mike proclaimed.

"I didn't sign up for all this PDA crap tonight." He groaned and took a long pull from his beer.

"They're newlyweds. Remember how we were?" Macy asked him.

"Why would you say that?" Daniel asked, finishing his beer and opening another. "Nope, don't need that thought."

David was struggling to hold a straight face, but mostly failing. She watched as he lost his internal fight to hold it in and slapped his knee in his fit of laughter.

"Oh, this is real funny," Daniel said drily.

Mike began to shake, and she looked down to find him silently chuckling, hiding his face behind her. "I am not going to hide you," she told him, and stood.

"Come on, Kristen, we can check on Chris and bring dinner out to these fools." Macy led the way into the house.

Kristen didn't stop the screen door from slamming as she went in. As soon as she and Macy made it into the living room, they both lost it. She wiped her eyes, trying to contain the fits of laughter.

"Men," Macy said and threw her hands up in confusion.

"They do love to give each other a hard time," Kristen agreed.

They checked on Chris, and Kristen helped him quickly with his math homework as Macy got the rest of the food out of the oven. It didn't take long, and they all joined the men on the back porch again.

"I need to talk to you Kristen." Daniel stood, and gestured with his crutch to the house.

"Now?" She huffed, but went back inside again. "What?"

"There is a rumor going around that this wasn't a real wedding, and I want you to be honest with me," Daniel told her.

"A rumor? How did you even hear it? You never leave the house!"

She was giving in to her frustration and only lowered her voice because she remembered Chris was within earshot. "Yes, we got married, like for real married."

"I just wanted you to know, and I didn't want to say something in front of everyone."

"Like her husband?" Mike asked, stepping into the kitchen.

"Well, yeah," Daniel answered. "I didn't think she'd be honest if you were with her." His honest answer had Kristen sucking in a breath and holding it, waiting for Mike's reaction.

"I didn't trick her into anything if that's what you're insinuating." Mike dropped one arm over her shoulders. "I love her, and you're going to have to get used to it."

"Love?"

She nodded, watching as Daniel dropped himself into a chair at the table. "Daniel, don't be dramatic." She pretended to whisper to Mike, "I think we know where Chris is getting it from."

Mike smiled but didn't look at her, keeping his eyes on Daniel.

"You're being honest?" Daniel was looking at Mike, like she wasn't even there.

Mike gave him one nod, and she watched as something unspoken passed between the men.

"Well, shit, guess I'm stuck with you for life now?" Daniel didn't look as annoyed as he had earlier, and she hoped that was a good sign.

"Forever, bro," Mike answered.

Daniel nodded, and they stood there as he went back to the group outside.

"I missed the beginning, what'd he say?" Mike asked.

"Someone is spreading rumors that we aren't really married." She sighed.

"What the fuck? At this point we should just tape our certificate up at the diner for everyone to see." He shook his head.

"Small town problems."

"Small town busybodies."

"Come on, let's eat." She took his hand and pulled him back out.

They had just started to eat when Kristen's phone rang. She pulled it out of her pocket, not recognizing the number, and answered it.

"Hello?" she asked.

"Where is my son?" She heard Sharon screech through the phone.

She cut her eyes at Mike to confirm he did hear it. He reached for the phone, but she shook her head instead.

"He's busy at the moment, can I take a message?" She wasn't letting this woman ruin their night.

"You put him on the phone. Now!" The last rivaled a toddler temper tantrum on pitch.

"I'm sorry, but as I stated, he is busy. Can I help you with something?"

"There is nothing you can help me with. Nothing."

With that last bit of venom, Sharon ended the call. Kristen quickly saved the number before putting her phone down on the table.

"I'm sorry," Mike told her.

"What was that about?" Daniel asked.

She waited for Macy to tell him to mind his business, but she looked just as curious.

"My mother wants me to marry Beth still," Mike answered.

"But you're already married?" Macy asked.

"No one seems to want to accept that. Which is likely where the rumors are coming from." She played with the label on her bottle of water as everyone took that in.

"This is ridiculous." Mike drained his beer and stood. "I'll be right back." He kissed Kristen on the top of her head and walked into the house.

"His mother called his father, and they both keep referring to me as his first wife. It's getting him upset, and we can't seem to get them to listen or leave us alone."

"She needs to go home," Macy commented.

"Mike told her to get out of his house today. We don't know yet if she did or if she's going home, but that tells me she's likely still there," Kristen admitted.

"Excuse me." David's suddenly serious tone shocked everyone.

He stood and went in the house, following Mike.

"Sorry, everyone," Kristen told them.

"Can I be excused to?" Chris asked.

"Let's go get you ready for bed." Macy walked in with him, leaving Daniel and Kristen on the porch alone.

"Is it worth all this?" he asked. There was no sarcasm in his tone, only concern.

Kristen nodded and then rested her head on the table to hide the tears she'd been fighting every time she thought about how much drama this was causing in Mike's family.

"Okay." Daniel situated his crutches and stood. "Let's go."

"Go?" She brought her head up, wiping tears. "Where?"

"To find your husband and discuss how to fix this."

Daniel waited as she opened the door for him to walk inside. They found Mike and David out front by Mike's truck. Mike was on the phone angrily yelling at someone.

"He's been doing this since I walked out here. I think it's his father now," David told them.

"I hate that this is my fault." Kristen hugged herself and watched as Mike yelled at the phone.

"It's not your fault. Mike and his father have never gotten along, same with his mother," Daniel reassured her. "Mike wouldn't be with that Beth chick no matter if you were in the picture or not, I promise."

Kristen nodded but wondered if their marriage was causing more problems for him than he would have been prepared to deal with. She wondered if he wanted to stay married at this point. All she'd done so far was help drive a wedge between him and his family.

Mike hung up the phone and mimicked tossing it into the woods. He didn't, but he wanted to.

"Would you mind staying here tonight?" Mike asked David.

"It's no problem," he answered.

"I'm going to have to do something to get her out of my place. She apparently moved Beth's mother in with her." He pulled at his hair and came away with a clenched fist. "I don't know what to do at this point," he admitted.

"We can call the police, maybe have them issue a warning that she needs to get out?" Daniel offered.

"I threatened it, but I'd really like to not have to take it there. It looks like I'm going to have to though." Mike sighed.

"Well, I need to put the utilities in my name, so why not just call tomorrow and cut them off?" David offered. "It's a bit of a long game, but if Daniel doesn't mind me crashing here for a few nights, I can wait to move in."

"You know you're welcome here," Daniel assured.

"That's genius." Mike smiled.

Kristen stood there, watching the men plot to get rid of Mike's mother and feeling horrible about the whole situation. It was her fault things were getting to this point with his family.

She folded her arms across her chest as the guys continued to talk, lost in her own thoughts and misery over the situation.

"Kristen." Mike pulled her from her thoughts. "Are you okay?"

"I'm fine," she replied automatically.

"I think we're going to go," Mike told Daniel and ushered Kristen to the truck.

"We can stay," she protested, but she didn't have it in her to make it convincing.

Mike didn't respond, just opened the door for her and helped her up. She didn't protest further.

When they were out of the driveway and on their way home, Mike finally spoke. "What's going on?"

"Nothing."

"Kristen, something is up. I can't help if I don't know," he pleaded.

"I just feel bad. This is all my fault," she answered after a long pause.

"None of this is your fault."

"It feels like it."

"I promise it's not." He gripped the steering wheel until his knuckles turned white. "We will talk when we get home, okay? I don't want to do this while I'm driving."

She nodded, but there wasn't much he could say to really change things. If they hadn't started dating, it wouldn't have turned into this drama. If they hadn't decided to get married, even when it was pretend, then maybe he wouldn't be looking to force his mother out of his house.

20

———

Mike pulled into the driveway and threw the truck into park with a jerk. He wasn't about to let Kristen take the blame of his family bullshit. His family had always been a mess, and this was just par for the course on crazy. He wasn't even sure what his mother really hoped to gain by staying in his house.

"I'll come around and help you down," he told her.

"I've got it." Kristen opened the door and slid out of the truck, leaving her bag and other stuff behind as she shut the door.

It took him a moment to get himself in gear and get out of the truck completely. By then she was already unlocking the door.

"Kristen, look at me, please?" he asked as they walked in the house.

She did, but he could see the hurt in her eyes.

"Baby, please understand my family has been like this my entire life." He took her hands in his. "This is not because of you, it's because of them, and Beth."

Kristen nodded. "I'm going to go shower."

He let her go when she pulled her hands free. Dropping his hands to his sides, he stood there and watched her go and close the door behind her.

Once Kristen was out of sight, he pulled out his phone and called his mother.

"Mother."

"Yes?" She sounded so casual, like nothing was wrong.

"Where are you?"

"You know where I am Michael. Beth is here for dinner. We'd be happy to have you join us."

It took him a minute to unclench his hand from his phone. At this point he wasn't sure how it wasn't shattered simply from the grip he'd had on it with every conversation he'd had with her.

"I told you to leave," he said through gritted teeth.

"I don't have another place to stay here." She whined.

"Go stay with Beth if you must stay in town, but if you don't get out of that house tonight, I am calling the police." He waited for her to recover from her shocked gasp, as though he hadn't already told her. "Do not tempt me to do this, you have caused enough problems as it is, and if I ever see Beth or her mother again, I can promise you they will regret interfering with my relationship with Kristen."

"Michael, how dare you talk to me like this?" He heard the fear in her tone.

"I am not going to talk to you any other way. I don't want anything to do with you right now, and I am not sure I ever will. Get out of my house, and do not contact me again. Is that understood?"

"You can't mean that. You're just probably fighting with that—"

"I warned you once, don't you dare call *my wife* any names."

"Michael!" she yelled through the phone.

"If I want to speak to you then I will reach out, but don't count on it at this point." He pulled the phone away thinking to hang up, before changing his mind. "And if you contact my wife again, I will get a restraining order. The same goes for everyone else, so relay the message."

He hung up the phone and tossed it on the couch, falling down next to it. Now he needed to figure out how to fix things with Kristen. She was sensitive to other people's emotions, and this fighting with his mother was clearly getting to her.

He thought on that without coming up with much. The shower turned off, and after a minute or two, Kristen came out of the bathroom in her towel and looked down the hallway, finding him.

"Hey," she said, her voice hoarse, and despite the shower, he could see the splotches on her face, telltale signs that she had been crying.

"Kristen." He stood and walked to her.

"Mike."

"You are not the cause of any of this. It really has nothing to do with you, despite the way they are making it seem." He pulled her into his arms, breathing a sigh of relief when her arm came around him too. "Please, don't put this on you. I promise it's got nothing to do with you."

She backed up to face him, tears falling down her face. "I don't want to come between you and your family."

"You aren't."

The look she gave him told him she didn't believe him.

"Think about it. Have you ever heard me talk about my family?"

Kristen looked towards the ceiling, clearly thinking about it.

"It's never. I don't talk about my family; this rift was here long before you. I'm just sorry you have to be a part of it."

She blew out a breath. "Okay."

"Okay?"

She nodded and he bent down, hooking one arm behind her knees and the other around her back, scooping her up, and carrying her to the bedroom. He laid her on the bed and pulled the covers up over her, tucking her in.

"I'm going to go turn the lights off and lock up. I will be right back."

She didn't say a word, and he made quick work of making sure all the doors were locked and flipping the lights. When he came back to the room, she wasn't in bed where he left her.

"I couldn't sleep with my hair in a towel." She was sitting at her vanity, body still in a towel, but hair free and brushing it.

"Come to bed?" he asked, stripping his clothes as he walked to his side of the bed. Leaving his boxers on, he sat on the bed, facing her.

"I am," she told him.

He watched as she finished brushing her hair and put some lotion on her face. When she was done, she stood and walked towards him. At the edge of the bed, she reached to the top of her towel and let it fall to the ground.

She stood there in all her glory, facing him, letting him drink in the vision before him. He adjusted himself further down into the bed and waited to see what she would do next. With the emotions she'd thrown today, he didn't want to push her—she was in charge tonight.

"Mike?" she asked, and he could tell she was starting to doubt herself.

"You're in charge, Kristen. If you want to, we will; if not, I won't be mad."

"I wouldn't expect you to get mad about it. I trust and know you better than that."

With that affirmation, she put one knee on the bed, and then other, crawling over to him. He locked eyes with her, but his peripheral vision couldn't help but notice the way her breasts swayed as she did.

"I love you," he told her as she reached his face.

"I love you," she replied before bending down and taking his lips in the most passionate kiss they'd shared.

His already-hard cock pushed harder on the boxers he was wearing. He intended to let her take the lead, but his resolve was slipping as she continued to kiss him, her naked breasts brushing against his arm as she did.

She pulled her mouth away, both of them panting. "Take those off," she told him.

In a rush, he nearly fell off the bed, but he got them off and laid back down. Kristen climbed over him, he felt her wet heat immediately and his cock jumped at the excitement.

She stayed there for a moment, just looking at him. He watched her face as she slowly, carefully, slid down onto him until she had taken him fully.

A moan escaped her lips as she started to move. He watched, hands gripping the sheets to keep his hands off her as she moved and experimented on top of him. Willing himself to last longer, he gripped the sheets tighter, pulling them up some as he did.

"If you don't touch me soon, Mike..." She didn't finish.

He didn't need to hear anything else. His hands left the sheets, touching her everywhere at once. She cried out as he twisted her nipples, and he bucked beneath her, matching the rhythm she was setting.

Cupping the back of her neck, he pulled her face down to his, drinking her in, as a hand drifted to squeeze her ass. She whimpered a little as he squeezed and helped her find the pace they both needed tonight. He drove into her while guiding her body up and down as she grabbed the headboard for support.

"Mike!" she yelled.

"I love you, Kristen. Do you feel it?"

"Yes, yes, yes."

He felt her begin to clench him and finally let himself over the edge to join her. He loved this woman.

She crumpled on top of him, completely spent. "I love you, Mike."

Rolling off of him, she collapsed, sprawled out on the bed. Her breaths were still coming as quickly as his own.

"I love you too, Kristen."

He stood and went to the bathroom to clean himself up. He grabbed a washcloth for Kristen on his way back. When he returned, she tried to take it from him.

"Let me," he told her, and gently helped her clean up from their lovemaking.

Her blush excited him, and he wondered if it would for the rest of his life. Determined to find out, he tossed the cloth into the hamper and got in the bed, pulling her close to him. There was only one way to find out, he smiled to himself.

21

───────

They had been married for a few weeks now, and Kristen still got butterflies every time she saw Mike show up at the school to see her. The play was last night and had gone off without a hitch. The Pillars had pulled off a miracle of a fundraiser, and she'd nearly made as much as last year. Not bad, considering she had only a month to pull it off.

The silent auction was her idea and had pulled in the largest amount of the night, parents and neighbors eagerly bidding before the play. The kids had remembered their lines, and Mike's props had moved seamlessly onstage.

Mike's mother had come out to the house last week, surprising them both when she knocked. Mike hadn't invited her in, but she'd made an attempt at an apology from the porch and Kristen had accepted it readily. He was a tough sell, but they were back on speaking terms again.

As for Beth, she had opted not to renew her contract for next year. Kristen didn't like to wish bad things on anyone, but she had done a small dance at the news, hoping she'd found somewhere else to go.

"All of this?" Mike asked.

He was here today helping her pack up her room and get everything ready for next year. "Everything comes down," she told him.

"That's dumb. Why not just have everyone use the same rooms?"

"They have to get cleaned, and there is summer school and other things going on."

"It's still dumb." He grumbled but started taking posters off the wall.

"I have bins for everything we save. I would have asked Macy to help, but she's getting too big to do this kind of thing."

"She's tired too," he noted.

She smiled and touched her own stomach. She wasn't pregnant, and while she wasn't in a hurry to be, she also could picture perfectly the family they'd have one day.. One day she would be, and one day was enough for her.

"Let get it down so we can go home and get planning," he told her.

They had decided to take a trip this summer since she was off. It was going to be their honeymoon. They were planning to go soon so they could be back before Macy had the baby. Just in case though, David was sticking around so he could help with Chris if the baby came sooner than planned.

She backed up and took in the room and the man in it, thinking how much her life had changed in such a short time. She had never been this happy and couldn't wait to live this for the rest of her life.

ENGAGED TO HER NEIGHBOR
FINDING LOVE BOOK 1

He didn't want neighbors and she just wanted a fresh start.

Macy is starting over in a new town with her little brother to take care of. She settled on a small town where no one knows their past and they can be themselves without the shadow their father casts over them.

Daniel agreed to rent his property, but it was supposed to be simple instead, a kid and a dog interrupt his life from day one. Annoyed by the disturbance, he pushes them away until the day he really needs them.

When Daniel gets injured and Macy comes to the rescue, feelings get in the way. Macy agrees to help Daniel until he's recovered but never could have predicted that the arrival of Daniel's ex-fiance would lead to a fake engagement for herself.

Sparks fly when the town gets involved in the fake wedding and Macy and Daniel have to decide what they really want from each other. How far will they take this fake engagement? Can it become real?

CHAPTER 1
ENGAGED TO HER NEIGHBOR

What is going on? There was a kid in his yard, and a dog too. Daniel headed off his porch to investigate, leaning heavily on his cane. Today was not a good pain day and the last thing he needed to be doing was trekking across the yard in search of answers as to who the wayward dog and child belonged to.

He stopped and rubbed his knee as he made it to the bottom of the steps wincing as the pain shot up his leg before calming back down to its normal dull ache. The worst part was over until it was time to go back inside, stairs made the pain worse, walking more than just around his house was a close second to it.

The dog noticed him before the kid did and stopped chasing the ball and ran straight for Daniel. He braced for impact, but the dog stopped before reaching him and sniffed at him. He took in the yellow, almost white, dog before him. It was gentle, just inquisitive, sniffing him as though sizing him up as well. Daniel stuck his hand out for the dog to sniff and when he felt like he had received approval he patted the dog on the head that was almost reaching his waist and waited for the boy to approach.

\#

At least it wasn't raining, that was the only positive part of the day so far. Macy and her brother were supposed to be moving into the new house she had rented them today and everything that could go wrong so far, had. It was more stress than one person should have to deal with.

It all started when she tried to start the rented truck with all their belongings in it, of course the battery was dead. Skipping the costs on roadside assistance had seemed an easy way to save a few bucks, but it just figured she'd need it. Sixty bucks later she had paid someone to come out and jump the battery from the local tow company, and the rest of the day had been much the same. They got a late start, then she had to stop and get food for her and Chris because they had left the peanut butter and jelly sandwiches, that she had packed for them in her car, which of course was at the rental truck place.

The two-hour drive to their new home had been filled with traffic and two complete stops, taking them more than double what it should have. They were so far behind and now she needed to get everything out of the truck so she could return it tomorrow and get her car. She had only taken two days off for this move mentally and needed to get to finding a new job right away, plus she didn't want to pay for an extra day for the rental truck either.

Finally getting to the house which she had rented based off pictures online, she realized there was no way she was going to be able to back the truck down this long, narrow driveway, so now they were adding extra steps to everything. Now Chris had disappeared under the guise of taking Lucy, their lab, for a walk, leaving her to do it all on her own. Chasing him down would waste more time and honestly, he wasn't that much help, one trip to her three, but it was one less thing she had to carry at least.

Sighing, she set down the boxes she had carried in and went in search of Chris and Lucy. Yelling for him, she went through the small one-story house in search of them with no luck. Heading through the back door, she looked out into the yard for them, not seeing them anywhere. She yelled for them and heard Lucy bark, but no one came running. Deciding there was no hope for it, she stepped off the small back porch and went in the direction of the sound.

Looking around, she noticed that the pictures she had seen had done very little justice to the outdoor space here. There was just one neighbor, whose house she could just barely see from hers as it was a good walk away and sat higher than hers on a hill. It was that beautiful green hill that she climbed now. Whoever live here definitely took care of their yard because this was the greenest grass she had ever seen. It took considerable restraint on her part not to take off her shoes and see how it felt under her bare feet.

Smiling and slightly winded, she reached the top of the hill and looked upon a gorgeous two-story house made out of wood. This would be a perfect example of one of those log cabins from the shows on TV where people spend an insane amount of money building a vacation home that they intend to use only a few times a year.

Looking around she spotted Chris and Lucy with a man standing near the woods at the back of their properties. Macy cringed, as she knew how Chris felt about men with the way that their father had treated them. The boy was only eight and should have been running around without a care in the world, instead he was standing there head down, shuffling his feet and listening to the man talk. Lucy noticed her and came running over to greet her and walked with her to Chris.

I hope he hasn't made the new neighbors mad already. I hope that man isn't yelling at him either. Her head swirled with thoughts as she approached them.

The man was dressed in jeans and a solid grey t-shirt and was leaning on a cane with his left hand. He needed a haircut she noticed as she walked closer, it was past the point of touching his ears, but not long enough to be considered long hair. He had a full scruffy beard to match his brown hair that he was reaching up to scratch as she walked up. He looked like an untamed mountain man, one that definitely preferred to be left alone. The look he was giving her now definitely said that he didn't welcome distractions, especially in the form of a rambunctious dog and small boy.

"Hi, I'm Macy, we are moving in next door." She stuck out her hand to greet the man.

"Daniel, and I had guessed as much." He shook her hand. "I hope not to find everyone wandering around in my back yard now that you live here."

"No sir, I will make sure they know where the property line is." She put her hand on Chris's shoulder. "I'm sorry I was unloading the truck and I lost track of them."

The man looked at her. It was more than a look, it was a hard stare, taking her measure and clearly judging her parenting skills, finding them lacking. "See to it that you keep a better eye on them in the future."

With that the man turned and limped away, leaning heavily on his cane. She turned to Chris to fuss at him, but he still had his head down, clearly bothered by running into Daniel on his first day here.

"I'm sorry Macy, I didn't know I wasn't supposed to go this far."

"It's okay bud, you do now. If you had been helping though I would have been able to tell you after we got the truck unloaded."

Chris nodded and then headed down the hill towards their little house. Macy had decided it was in the best interest for both of them to move farther away from their hometown to get away from their father. He was in jail now for hitting a woman while he was driving drunk and injuring her pretty badly. She had lived, but barely. Even though he was locked up and they had nothing to do with it, the stigma of being Joe Manning's kids had followed them around before and had only gotten worse after the accident.

They had been treated as trash their whole lives simply because of parentage and their father hadn't treated them much better. She hadn't called him Dad in so long she had forgotten the last time she had. He wasn't a Dad; Joe was a drunk, and a mean one at that.

Macy's mom had passed away when she was too young to remember her well, then Joe had raised her, if you could call it that. She just remembered being alone all the time, and the endless string of neighbors that used to help watch her until Joe did something to make them stop watching her too. They moved around from trailer park to trailer park, sometimes only staying on someone else's couch because Joe never would hold down a job long.

Then Joe met Candice, or Candy as she was known to everyone else. How they managed to live together for nearly a year was something she never understood. Candy hadn't stuck around long after Chris was born, and then had just disappeared one day. From then on it had been Macy that took care of Chris.

She was only fifteen when he was born, it had made her scared to leave him with Joe while she went to school. Then she had come across an older neighbor that kept Chris for her while she was in school in exchange for Macy cleaning her house and helping her cook meals whenever she could.

It wasn't until she was a few years older and Ms. Mary had passed away that she realized Mary had just been protecting them and teaching Macy all the things that a mom would have taught her. She was their safe harbor in the storm that was their lives and Macy had cried like she had never done before when Ms. Mary had passed away. Joe had refused to take them to the funeral, which had also hurt.

She would have moved out then and tried to make her own way in the world instead of paying bills for Joe, but she couldn't do that to Chris. She had done her absolute best to keep him as sheltered from their father's violent tirades as she could, taking the brunt of his anger, but if she wasn't there anymore, it would all be at Chris.

Shortly after she turned 21, a lawyer contacted her; apparently Mary had a will and had put Macy in it. She had left her a nice sum of money but had decided that she couldn't know of it, or come into it until she was legally old enough to not have to give any to Joe. Ten thousand dollars was a lot of money then and Macy had thought hard about what to do with it.

It had been two years now and she was just reaching out to use it, starting with getting custody of Chris as soon as Joe's trial was over. Then they rented this house, paying for the deposit and a few months rent all at once. It gave her time to get settled into her new job before the big bill of rent was due, which was considerably more than they had been paying at the trailer. They would make it work though; she was sure of it.

They worked until past dark to get the truck unloaded and didn't have time to set anything up. Instead she and Chris curled up on their mattresses on the floor in sleeping bags once everything was in the house. She had found the small cooler with the sandwiches she had made yesterday for today's lunch in the back of the truck, making it so she didn't have to spend more money on food for the night.

She looked over at Chris, curled up with Lucy on his bed, hugging her protectively. She had been the one thing that made Chris feel safe, and she had always done her best to live up to that feeling. Lucy had bitten Joe once on his hand, he had cussed up a storm, but that was the last time he had ever attempted to hit Chris again, for which Macy had been grateful and rewarded Lucy with dinner scraps ever since, she had earned her place in their family.

Macy rolled onto her back and stared up at the ceiling, thinking about this decision. She hoped she could find a job and a sitter within the next two weeks or they were screwed. This plan had been thought out as intensely as she could with the exception of a job, she couldn't make the drive out here for interviews ahead of time, so she prayed that she would find one when Chris started school on Wednesday. With luck it would pay enough for her to only need to work during the day and not require her to get a sitter for after school.

Sleep wouldn't come and after laying there and worrying for too long, she got up and grabbed her cell phone before laying back down. Lucy had lifted her head to watch her but hadn't left Chris's side. Unlocking her phone, she started scrolling through the job postings for Allensville, VA.

FALLING FOR HER FAKE HUSBAND
FINDING LOVE BOOK 3 (COMING 2022)

He saved her once, but now she needs him again. This time, the stakes are higher...

Three years ago, Chloe was desperate to break-free from her controlling parents. Thankfully, her best friend David was willing to help her. It was only temporary after all. But what they thought would be a short-lived fake relationship ended with long-term consequences.

David did his part. He played the role. He left when it was time, even though it killed him to walk away. But after all these years, he still thinks about her and does his part to help her and the child they share.

Now, after doing everything she could to keep herself and her young daughter afloat, her parents want even more control. They want her daughter. Chloe refuses to let that happen, but she can't prevent it alone. She needs David's help.

When this young family reunites, what begins as a repeat of their fake relationship soon becomes something very real. Are Chloe and David ready to become a real family or are they wading into dangerous territory?

ABOUT THE AUTHOR

Toni Denise is a contemporary romance author who lives in Virginia with her husband, 4 kids, and 3 dogs. She enjoys reading as much as she does writing. She has 3 degrees in Business and works full time outside of her writing.

ALSO BY TONI DENISE

Westbeach Series (Amazon only, KU, and Print)

Old Friends

On the Run

One Last Chance

Out of Time

The Complete Westbeach Series

Finding Love Series (Available wide)

Engaged to Her Neighbor

Married to the Playboy

Falling For Her Fake Husband (coming 2022)

OLD FRIENDS
WESTBEACH SERIES BOOK 1

Sometimes a second chance can be the last chance.

Recently divorced, Kelly finds herself back in her hometown. Deciding that starting over is key, she and her son take to living a new life.

When a second chance with Mason, an old flame, ignites, Kelly is excited to feel love again.

But something is wrong. Someone is watching them, waiting to strike. Someone that knows them. Someone. . . close.

Not knowing who she can trust, Kelly is thrust into a life of fear and looking over her shoulder.

Where do you turn when the one person you thought you could trust might actually be the person you're running from?

A steamy romance novel with a moderate heat level.

CHAPTER 1
OLD FRIENDS

Taking in the scenery, Kelly wondered why she never came back to visit. Going home was hard, but it was only about a four-hour drive. She really should have come home before now. Taking the long road around the outside of town, the scenery alternated between trees so dense the automatic headlights came on in her car and open pastures with cows or horses in them. This time of year, everything was still bright green. It looked pretty, but she knew better; being late August, it was hot out there. Soon the brilliant green would give way to a wonder of colors as fall slowly crept in.

Turning the music down, she focused on the GPS and the last few miles of her trip. Traffic had started to pick up in the previous hour of her journey until she left the interstate. She was glad she had left earlier in the day; it was only about 4:00 p.m. now. A quick check of the back seat showed Hunter was waking up. For a seven-year-old, he wasn't a bad road-trip partner, but he had slept all but the first hour, when he ate most of the snacks. "Hey, Hunt, we're almost there. Are you excited?"

"Are we in a zoo?" Hunter sleepily asked.

Kelly took another look around, wondering why this was even a question. Cows. There were cows on both sides of the road. "No, baby, there are ranches around here that raise cows."

"So, I'll see the zoo every day?"

"Yes." Simpler to agree than to explain more as he wasn't awake yet. Besides, in all his seven years, he'd never seen the countryside, and Westbeach was about as opposite of DC as you could get.

As they made the last turn, the woods on either side were a welcome presence, adding shade to the last bit of the trip, which had been mostly on the sunny highway. She was going to have a sunglasses tan for sure. Finally pulling in to the driveway, Kelly breathed a sigh of relief to see her aunt and uncle already there and waiting for them.

The light blue house was one level and had a small new porch on the front. The wood was still white looking, so she could tell it hadn't been there long. The front yard was freshly cut, and there were trees on both sides of the property and behind it. A privacy fence, which also looked new, wrapped around the backyard. No neighbors could be seen unless you were in the road. *Wonder if I'll be able to sleep without the noise of the city?*

Aunt Mary was the first to come off the porch as Kelly parked the car. Mary, in her signature flower dress and floppy hat over her white hair, had always been able to style anything except herself. Her dresses were like something older ladies probably wore in the fifties. Gardening, cooking, shopping—same dresses; some things never changed. Bob, on the other hand, was a jeans and T-shirt man. Kelly could never remember Uncle Bob having hair—on his head or face. Much like Mary though, his style was the same no matter what he was doing. The only thing these two changed was the colors each day.

When Kelly stepped out of her car, Aunt Mary immediately wrapped her in a welcoming hug. "How are you doin', dear? How was the trip?"

"Let her get out of the car, Mary." Uncle Bob always sounded a tad sour but was a sweetheart underneath.

"I am, I am." Aunt Mary backed up and opened the back door for

Hunter to climb out of the car. "Hunter! You've gotten so big!" Hunter grinned and stood tall at her praise. Mary ruffled his hair and proceeded to go to the trunk with Uncle Bob to get their bags. "Is this all you brought, honey?"

"For now. The rest is packed, and Dylan is supposed to send it this week, but we'll see if he remembers to let the movers in or not."

"Okay, let us know if you forgot anything." Aunt Mary smiled sadly at Kelly.

"You know I will." She plastered on a big smile to reassure everyone that she really was okay. Taking Hunter's hand, she turned and walked into the house.

When she walked in, the first thing she noticed was that the house was fully furnished; some things even looked new. A gray sofa in the living room faced a flat-screen TV with a small coffee table. Passing through the living room to the kitchen, she noticed there was a cherry-colored table for four with a bouquet of fresh flowers waiting for them. *Definitely Aunt Mary's idea.* And the smell—some version of every spice, but in a good way—was just like Bob and Mary's house. It was a welcoming scent, the smell of home.

Kelly walked down the hall of the modest one-story house, pulling her suitcase behind her. Three rooms, two bathrooms—per Mary's directions, hers was the last on the left. The room had a large queen-sized bed in the center with a gorgeous purple quilt and matching pillows on it. A dresser sat against the long wall with a mirror attached.

Checking all the doors, she discovered the closet was behind the open bedroom door, and against the wall was a master bath. A purple shower curtain hung already with silver bath mats. Aunt Mary really should have been an interior designer, and her remembering Kelly's favorite color just made it that much better.

Kelly had never been able to have everything decorated in her favorite color before, but now she could do her thing. Putting her bag down she took a deep breath; divorce wasn't going to be too bad if this was how it started. Coming back home wasn't all that bad, even if it did make her feel a little like a failure for her marriage not working.

There was no love lost in her marriage anyway. Dylan didn't even fight for custody of Hunter. He just let them go and agreed to everything—not that she had asked for much, just child support and custody. Dylan didn't even want weekends with Hunter. Kelly sighed as she looked in the mirror and pulled her hair into a ponytail before heading back out to the other three noisily chatting about cows in the dining room.

"Hunter tells me he's excited to see the zoo every day," Uncle Bob informed her with a laugh as he pulled Kelly up for a quick hug. Although pushing seventy, Bob was still a tall man. He was the exact opposite of Mary, who was shorter than Kelly by five inches, standing at five feet tall. The family had always joked that it was her hat that gave her an inch or two and that she genuinely was less than five feet. Mary had always laughed along as well, shushing everyone, but never argued it.

"Something tells me he'll eventually tire of it," Kelly said with a small laugh of her own.

"I stocked some essentials in the cabinets and fridge; wasn't sure what all you would need. We can go to dinner later, or you can come over and I'll cook." Aunt Mary always made sure everyone had eaten. If you weren't hungry, she was going to have you doing something until you were. "We are waiting on the handyman though. The disposal isn't working right now."

"No problem, and we can eat whatever is easiest for you tonight. Thank you guys again." Bending down, she hugged Aunt Mary again and gave her a kiss on the cheek. "I don't know what I would do without you guys here."

"Family helps family, dear." And that was all Aunt Mary was going to say about it. No thanks needed ever.

"I love you." Before either of them did more than tear up, Kelly changed the subject. "The handyman? Is that who redid the front porch? It looks nice."

"Yes, yes. Bob thought he was going to do it. Took the boards off and then decided it was too much for one old man, like I said." She cut a look at Bob, who decided not to say anything and continued to talk to Hunter. "Thankfully," Mary continued, "the handyman was able to get out here and get it done before you got here."

"Really?" Hunter shouted and jumped up from the table to run out the back door.

"I told him there was a swing set out there." Bob smiled and moved to follow Hunter out the door.

"He will never come inside again." Kelly laughed and moved to the window to see Hunter happily swinging while Uncle Bob looked on.

"Go unpack, and I'll wait right here for the doorbell," Mary said while shooing Kelly from the window. "He'll be fine."

"I know. I'll be in his room for now if you need me."

Wandering down the hall, Kelly opened the door across from her room and was pleased to find an office. Mary really had thought of everything. A small desk sat facing the window with a fancy-looking high-backed office chair, and she could see the entire backyard from there. A tall lamp in the corner would keep her from having to turn on the overhead light to see, and a ceiling fan was a nice addition. The room was painted a darker shade of blue, but it didn't seem to make the room feel smaller.

There was plenty of room left in there for her treadmill since there was no gym here that she knew of, and going for a run would be difficult with Hunter still home for the summer. Mary always knew what worked and what didn't without even trying. Kelly would be glad to get back to work in two weeks in her new office. Thankfully, her legal transcription was work from home, and they had been generous with her time off under the circumstances. She would have a pile of work when she got back to it though. It was going to be rough going back to work after all this time off. Thinking about her emails that she hadn't checked all day, she walked out of the room and closed the door.

Moving on, Kelly checked the room next to hers and saw a twin bed, some toys already set out for Hunter, and a large baseball poster

　　　　　　　　Chapter 1

on the wall across from her. Smiling, she walked over and touched it, amazed by the little things Bob and Mary had thought of to help Hunter adjust. She'd also bet money that there was no swing set here before Kelly decided to move in. Kelly heaved Hunter's suitcase on the bed and started to unpack and put away the clothes.

"I didn't pack hangers." Kelly let out a deep sigh. "If this is the worst part, I'm good, right?" Musing to herself, she walked down the hall to see if Mary wanted to go to the store. "Mary, are you interested in running to the—" Seeing a man in the kitchen, Kelly stopped midsentence.

"Kelly, this is Mason, the handyman. Mason, do you remember Kelly?"

"How could I forget?" Drying his hands off, he looked up, and Kelly stared into eyes she hadn't seen in twelve years. Mason Cole.

"Wow! How are you? It's been forever." Not sure what to do with herself, she leaned awkwardly against the wall, taking in this man who had been a teenager when she saw him last. Instead, here was this man with his dark brown hair and muscles she could see through his blue shirt. And those blue eyes... a woman could get lost in those eyes. He hadn't changed much other than getting older, like her she supposed. He was still as handsome as ever.

"How's the set working out?" Mason interrupted Kelly's assessment of him. Oh, that smile, crooked with one dimple on the right cheek. That smile could make women fall all over themselves to get a glimpse of it. Nope, that hadn't changed one bit.

"Hunter is already out there." Mary saved her from having to form an answer. Nothing could have prepared Kelly for seeing this man in her kitchen.

Swallowing down old feelings and trying to move forward, Kelly shifted to look out the window on the back door to see Hunter still outside playing. Taking it in for the first time, she noticed the back deck was only slightly above ground level, just one step up. *I need to get a table and chairs for out here, so I can work and watch Hunter play.* The yard was a fair size, plenty of room for Hunter to run around, and the start of the tree line had been fenced into the yard, giving him a shaded place to play. The swing set was a good size as well, containing two swings, a slide, and monkey bars on one end. Uncle Bob strolled from the deck to the yard, watching Hunter wear himself out. *At least he'll sleep tonight, even after that long nap in the car.*

"What did you need, dear?" Aunt Mary asked.

"Oh, I didn't pack hangers and was wondering where the closest store was?" She focused on Mary, anything to not stare at this too-hot-to-be-here man in the kitchen.

"That would still be Gersham's down on Main Street. I have to head there to order the part for your disposal if you'd like a ride?" Of course, it was Mason who answered. And a ride, really? Lord knew she wanted to go for a ride. Wait, where had that thought come from? How unlike her; must be the nerves.

"I don't want to impose. I can head down there later."

"No imposing at all. Grab your bag and hop in the truck." Interesting how the words he chose said he made the decision, but the tone made it clear it was still her call.

Grabbing her bag, she let Hunter know she would be right back. For all he cared though, he was still enthralled with the swings and slide out back. After hugging Aunt Mary, she walked out to the dark blue Dodge Ram sitting in her driveway. Mason was standing by the truck and opened the door for her. He waited until she had settled before closing it. *What am I supposed to say now? What do I do?* Placing her bag in her lap, she sat still as he climbed in and backed out the driveway. Not much was said on the way to the store.

Staring out the passenger window, she watched the scenery. Everything seemed the same, and yet it all seemed so different at the same time. When they got to the store, they went their separate ways after Mason pointed her in the right direction. She grabbed several packs of hangers and headed toward the checkout.

Mason was already standing there putting in an order for whatever part it was he needed.

As she approached, a shiver ran down her spine. Kelly felt like someone was watching her. Looking around, she didn't see anyone else in the store besides Mason and the clerk. Still, she picked up her pace, unable to shake the creepy feeling. She set the hangers on the counter, continuing to look around while waiting for them to finish. *You're losing it. No one is in here, just the empty store getting you creeped out.*

Needing a distraction, she watched the interaction going on at the register. The woman was practically hanging on Mason's every word like she was super interested in garbage disposals. Kelly rolled her eyes. When she looked up again, Mason winked at her. She had been caught. Completely distracted from the creepy feeling, she now had a new one—full-on embarrassment.

Part ordered and hangers paid for, they walked back to the truck again. Mason took the awkward bags of hangers and opened her door for her. While Kelly buckled in, he put the bags in the back seat, then shut her door and got in.

"Didn't like her much, did you?"

Kelly felt the heat creep up her face. He wasn't going to ignore her eye roll. "It wasn't that. More of a disbelief type of thing." *There, that makes me sound less rude for not liking someone I don't even know and positively not jealous.*

"Nope, it's been a while, but you still can't hide anything. It's all over your face," he teased.

Kelly put her hand to her heart and leaned toward Mason, doing an exaggerated impersonation of the busty clerk. "Oh, please tell me more about garbage disposals." She batted her lashes. "I just don't know what I would do without you having come in today, Mason." Kelly laughed and sat back right in the seat.

"Pretty good impression actually. Now you know why I didn't want to go to the store alone." Mason cut her a sly look but laughed as well. After a moment, they both fell into a companionable silence for the rest of the trip. Pulling up, Mason stopped her from opening the door with a hand on her shoulder. "It's good to see you and have you home again, even if it's not under the best of circumstances."

"Thank you. I'm glad to be home. No love lost in the reason for my coming home, so no worries. I'm glad I got to see you."

"If you need anything while you're here, let me give you my number. Your aunt and uncle call when something needs to be done in one of their rentals. Most of your new home has been newly renovated though; they really went all out to make it right for you. Oh, and I'll let Bob know when the part comes in. She said Tuesday, but when I pick it up will depend on when I can get someone to go to the store with me." Mason laughed again.

"I noticed. The porch looks great, and the swing set too. If you let me know when the part is ready, I can run in and pick it up, and then you can avoid the store altogether." Kelly winked at him. "You can just let me know. Let me find a paper, and I'll give you my number." She dug through her bag and came up with a crayon and a receipt. Blushing again at how much of a mess she must seem, she wrote her number down and handed it to him. Saying their good-byes, she hopped out of the truck and went inside with a smile on her face.

#

Kelly Marie Holstead, he didn't know she would be there today. He could have sworn it was tomorrow that Mary said she would get here. Pulling into his own driveway, he smiled as he remembered Kelly's reaction to Darlene, the clerk at Gersham's. Just like the old Kelly would have done, she let loose with that cute little eye roll. Heading inside, he greeted Shep, his aging yellow lab, with a pat on the head. Shep followed him through the house, waiting to be let outside. Grabbing a beer from the fridge, Mason opened the back door and went out to the deck, Shep in tow.

Checking his phone, he texted Nate, his brother and business partner, about the disposal and the part needed. He pulled Kelly's crayon-written number out of his pocket and plugged it into his phone. *Should I text her now, so she has my number? Is it too soon?* After deciding to just program the number in and debate it later, his thoughts wandered to the day he had. After a rough morning with two young guys late to work, again, he was frustrated and cranky when he remembered he was supposed to check on Kelly's disposal today. When he pulled up, he was in no mood for small talk with Mary but had resigned himself to it. Then he noticed another car in the driveway.

Kelly apparently hadn't been expecting him. He wasn't entirely expecting her either. He hadn't seen her in almost twelve years, since they were seventeen and about to graduate high school. That summer was some of the best memories he had though. Kelly was his best friend, but when they went to college in different states, they had slowly lost touch. It was one of his biggest regrets. He and Kelly had shared everything—sometimes too much, but he could always tell her anything, and she, him. He knew Kelly had gotten married right after she graduated college, and that was about it.

She still looked as good as ever, a more mature woman and no longer the body of a teenager, but time had been kind to her. Her blonde hair had been pulled back, but it was more than shoulder length and had some highlights. Her body though, she looked like she took care of herself; he could see her defined leg muscles under her shorts. Her curves were more significant than he remembered. She wore no makeup, probably not something she usually did, but no reason to get dolled up for a road trip to move. He liked the no makeup look though, no pretending, nothing to hide.

Just then his phone went off, pulling him out of his thoughts as they headed in the wrong direction. Texting Nate back, he got up, adjusted his pants, and Shep followed him in the door. Nate was going to give him a hard time about seeing Kelly, and about venturing into Gersham's when he knew Darlene would be working. He wasn't kidding; he had taken Kelly as a bit of a buffer. Darlene always shamelessly threw herself at him, but she'd limit it to flirting if there was someone else in the store. The woman never took the hint that he wasn't interested, even though he had tried to let her down gently many times before. Now he just avoided the place when he knew she was working.

Time to make dinner. Pulling out the chicken, he got started on cooking. *Wonder if she still cooks as well as she used to?* What the hell was he doing, thinking about her so much? It had only been a few minutes, and nothing had even happened to make him feel so much about her. She hadn't thrown herself at him like most women, so what was it?

Finishing up dinner, he carried it to the living room. Watching TV would distract his wayward thoughts.

\#

He waited in his car with the lights off until Mason had finally left Kelly's house. He had watched her from the back of the store as she searched hangers. He couldn't believe she had been home just a few hours and was already back with Mason. How had that happened? Had to be her meddling aunt. He had been watching the house for the past week waiting for her arrival and would meet her again soon. She was supposed to come back after she finished school, and like a fool, he had expected her to, but no, she went and got married and hadn't come back at all.

He had followed her online for a long time and had made sure she found out about her husband's cheating. Chuckling to himself, he remembered how easy that had been. He had just pretended to be the secretary's doctor and called their house phone looking for the father of the baby. Of course, Kelly had answered. Then he "accidentally" spilled the news of the baby to her. He had gotten her home now. She hadn't been happy in her marriage anyway, so he didn't feel bad. This time, she would be his, and neither Mason nor anything else was going to stand in his way. He carefully put away his phone, excited to have new photos of her on it, and headed home.